"Do you know that you smell like a forest after a rainstorm?" Luke whispered, unable to keep the words inside him any longer. "All fresh and clean, but tangled and a little wild."

"Is that good?" Sarah whispered back.

He heard a slight tremor in her voice and saw a haze of desire clouding her bewitching green eyes. She was caught fast in the same honeyed spell that he was.

"Very good," he assured her, then reached up and stroked the dark silk of her hair, loving the sound of the small catch in her breathing. Recalling how her ex-husband had trampled on her sweetness made him madder than he'd been in a long time.

She felt him stiffen. "Is something wrong?"

"No, I was just thinking of that mule-stupid guy you married—he must have been crazy to let you go."

She smiled, but it was forced. "That's kind of you to say—"

Luke grabbed her and turned her to face him. "Listen to me. I am not being kind, I have never been kind where beautiful women are concerned, and I'm not about to start now—"

"Beautiful?" she asked in a hushed voice. "You think I'm beautiful?"

He made a sound of exasperation. "What in blazes do they teach you in the city? Yes, I think you're beautiful, and not just because of the way you look. There's a decency, a goodness in you that makes you seek out people in need." He lifted a hand to her cheek and brushed her flushed skin with reverence. "You don't need all those bottles and jars, Sarah. Your beauty shines out from inside you. . . ."

WHAT ARE *LOVESWEPT* ROMANCES?

They are stories of true romance and touching emotion. We believe those two very important ingredients are constants in our highly sensual and very believable stories in the LOVESWEPT line. Our goal is to give you, the reader, stories of consistently high quality that may sometimes make you laugh, sometimes make you cry, but are always fresh and creative and contain many delightful surprises within their pages.

Most romance fans read an enormous number of books. Those they truly love, they keep. Others may be traded with friends and soon forgotten. We hope that each LOVESWEPT romance will be a treasure—a "keeper." We will always try to publish

LOVE STORIES YOU'LL NEVER FORGET
BY AUTHORS YOU'LL ALWAYS REMEMBER

The Editors

THE LAST AMERICAN HERO

RUTH OWEN

BANTAM BOOKS

NEW YORK · TORONTO · LONDON · SYDNEY · AUCKLAND

THE LAST AMERICAN HERO
A Bantam Book / March 1994

*LOVESWEPT and the wave design are registered
trademarks of Bantam Books, a division of
Bantam Doubleday Dell Publishing Group, Inc.
Registered in U.S. Patent
and Trademark Office and elsewhere.*

*All rights reserved.
Copyright © 1994 by Ruth Owen.
Cover art copyright © 1994 by Hal Frenck.
No part of this book may be reproduced or transmitted
in any form or by any means, electronic or mechanical,
including photocopying, recording, or by any
information storage and retrieval system, without
permission in writing from the publisher.
For information address: Bantam Books.*

*If you purchased this book without a cover you should be aware that this
book is stolen property. It was reported as "unsold and destroyed" to the
publisher and neither the author nor the publisher has received any
payment for this "stripped book."*

*If you would be interested in receiving protective vinyl covers for your
Loveswept books, please write to this address for information:*

> *Loveswept
> Bantam Books
> P.O. Box 985
> Hicksville, NY 11802*

ISBN 0-553-44426-3

Published simultaneously in the United States and Canada

*Bantam Books are published by Bantam Books, a division of Bantam Dou-
bleday Dell Publishing Group, Inc. Its trademark, consisting of the words
"Bantam Books" and the portrayal of a rooster, is Registered in U.S. Patent
and Trademark Office and in other countries. Marca Registrada. Bantam
Books, 1540 Broadway, New York, New York 10036.*

PRINTED IN THE UNITED STATES OF AMERICA

OPM   0 9 8 7 6 5 4 3 2 1

To Pam Baker,
who shares my love for cowboys,
and to Beth de Guzman,
who helped me to write a "big" story

ONE

"Luke Tyrell?"

Christ, not another one, Luke thought as he settled more deeply into the corner of the graffiti-scarred booth in the back of Bubba's Bar and Grill. He'd hoped to find some peace in this smoke-filled dive, hoped no one would bother him here. It worked, up to a point. The patrons weren't the kind to engage in social banter, unless it was over tattoos or the latest centerfold in *Hustler*. But he'd forgotten about the women, the ones who trolled places like this for customers. Three had approached him so far this evening, and now another one was standing at the table. He was getting damn tired of this. He pulled his broad-brimmed Stetson down more firmly over his eyes, hoping the action would let the lady know that he wasn't interested.

It didn't.

"You are Luke Tyrell, aren't you?"

Persistent cuss, he thought. That and the sweetly husky quality in her voice made him almost curious enough to lift up his hat and take a look at her. Almost. "Listen, darlin'," he said in a low, languid baritone, "I'm sure you do what you do real well. Another time I might take you up on it, but tonight I'm just not interested."

"Well, that's swell, cowboy, because neither am I."

This wasn't the response he'd expected. Tipping up his hat, he took a quick look at the woman who'd refused to leave him in peace. Then he took a closer look.

She wasn't a hooker. She wasn't dressed for the part. Her worn down-vest and baggy jeans discouraged desire rather than inviting it, and her oversize work shirt effectively hid every aspect of her figure from her neck to her waist. Her thick dark hair was cut in a simple style, with a fringe of bangs covering her forehead and the rest pulled back by some sort of clip. From this angle Luke couldn't tell whether it was long or short, straight or curly. And he couldn't tell what shade it was, for the nuances of color were lost in the dimly lighted room. At first glance she seemed deceptively ordinary, the kind of woman he'd pass on the street and not look at twice. Then he saw her eyes.

Their color, too, was obscured by the dim light. But color didn't matter. Her eyes burned into him, demanding attention the way a hawk demands attention of a dove. Beneath her baggy clothes and schoolgirl haircut, the lady was a predator. Others might miss the look, but Luke knew it. He saw it every time he looked in a mirror.

After seeing those eyes of hers, he found himself half-wishing that she *were* a hooker.

"Are you going to ask me to sit down?"

Not a chance, Luke thought, his common sense asserting itself. This lady was trouble. He could smell it. He could taste it. And he'd had about all the trouble he could stand for one day. "Look, ma'am, all I want to do is finish my beer in peace and be on my way out of town. So if you don't mind—"

"This won't take long, I promise," she said, as she slid into the other side of the booth. She sat in an unexpectedly modest fashion, ramrod straight with her hands resting out of sight in her lap. Her manner might be demure, but she was not. "I have a proposition for you," she said straight out.

Luke pushed up his hat a little farther, interested in spite of himself. "Proposition?" he echoed, his tone sizzling with suggestion.

Even in the faint light he could see her blush. "Not *that* kind of proposition," she said. Watching her face, he could almost see the thoughts running through her mind, the sudden knowledge of the image she must present to him—an unattached woman approaching an unattached man in a bar, and using the word "proposition." Embarrassed, she dropped her gaze. He experienced a keen, unexpected feeling of loss.

Still not looking at him, she continued, "I heard

you got turned down for a job at the Providence today."

"Well, you heard wrong," Luke said, bristling. "I was the one who did the turning down. The place was a little too, uh, religious for my taste."

She lifted her head, and he could see that her eyes were brimming with mischief.

"Brennermen does thump that Bible pretty loud, doesn't he?" she asked.

"Pound is more like it. Community prayer in the morning and before bed at night. Grace at every meal, and required attendance at Sunday services." Luke took off his hat and plowed his strong fingers through his hair in a quick, frustrated motion. "Made me think I was signing up for the clergy instead of for a stockman position."

"The money's good," she pointed out.

"Freedom's better," he countered. "I like to choose where and when I worship." He studied his hat, running a finger along its well-worn brim. "Kind of like the way I choose where and when I want company. Now's not one of those times. So if you don't mind, Mrs. . . . ?"

"Gallagher. Sarah Gallagher. I own the Corners Ranch just north of town, and before you tell me to go away again, I want you to know that I'm here to offer you a job."

Lord, she got out more words in a single breath than most people did in a minute. "No offense, but shouldn't your husband be here doing the asking?"

"You have problems doing business with a woman?"

"Damn straight," he said. "Any smart man would."

Her eyes snapped fire at his comment. She'd like to throttle him, Luke thought, amused. But his amusement turned to respect as she visibly reined in her anger. Luke had a short fuse himself, and he knew how hard it was to snuff out a fire once it was started. This lady appeared to have more than her share of fire. . . .

She was talking again. "It's a good job. I can't offer you as much money as Brennermen did, but I'll provide your room and board. And," she said, a smile replacing her frown, "I'll make sure I keep my Bible out of your sight."

That damn smile of hers could get him in a world of trouble. Her nature might be ornery as a mountain cat, but her lips were soft and inviting, with a naughty playfulness that put him in mind of a kitten. Warning bells rang faintly in his head. "So why isn't your husband here?" he repeated, more sternly this time.

"I'm not married."

Warning bells turned to sirens. "Not interested," he said, fighting the sudden roughness in his throat.

"But you haven't even heard the details."

"I don't have to," he stated. The last thing he needed in his life was an unattached female with an intriguing smile and eyes that blazed like stars in the heavens. He liked his relationships short and uncomplicated and did his best to keep them that way. But eyes like hers could start him thinking about settling down, about caring for something—and someone. And that was a risk he wasn't prepared to take again, for anyone.

He settled back against the scarred wall of the booth and pulled his hat back down over his eyes. "I've been offered a job on an oil rig. There's three hundred miles of highway between here and Houston, and I'm planning to drive it straight through. I'd appreciate a little quiet so I can rest up a bit before I take off. Good night, Miss Gallagher."

He figured she'd leave, that she'd slip out of his booth and his life, leaving him a little emptier for the loss of her sweet lips and bright eyes. He figured wrong. She stood up and reached over the table, whipping off his hat in a single swipe.

Nobody, but nobody, touched Luke Tyrell's hat. He rose slowly, straightening until his lean six-foot-six frame topped her head by at least a foot. "Give that back," he said with true menace.

"Not until you've listened to me," she said.

She held the hat behind her, out of his immediate reach. Another woman might mistake the extent of his rage and use the gesture as a childish, coy flirtation. But Luke saw the tightness in her jaw and knew she was fully aware of his anger and willing to face it. Once again he accorded her a measure of grudging respect.

"I need your help, Mr. Tyrell. I've tried, but I can't manage my place all alone. So far I've kept it going on a wing and a prayer, but I've learned the county building inspector's going to examine it in sixty days. If I haven't been able to make the necessary repairs by then . . ."

Her eyes completed the sentence, staring up into his in a desperate plea for help. *Green,* he thought. Green as the deep, secret heart of a forest. Gazing into them, he saw beneath her tough exterior to the soft, vulnerable center of her soul. Somewhere near his own heart a string pulled taut. She's scared, he thought, so scared, she's willing to show her fear to me. The few minutes he'd known her had showed him that she was a proud, strong-willed woman, used to meeting and besting life's challenges on her own. Independent to a fault himself, Luke could imagine how much admitting her fear must have cost her.

"Surely, there's someone around here who can help you."

"There's no one," she said flatly. The softness in her eyes died, hidden behind a condemning wall of disappointment. "No one in town will lift a finger to help me. You were pretty much my last hope."

For a moment he wondered if she was going to ask him again. And he wondered what his answer would be. The bright fire had left her, and her shoulders were slumped in defeat. Luke's experience had taught him that both men and women lied on a regular basis, but somehow he felt that she was telling the truth. She honestly believed he was her last hope.

From his vantage point he could see that her hair

was long, hanging down her back in a thick braid. He had a weakness for long hair, and for tough, stubborn ladies with expressive, vulnerable eyes. If she asked again, he might break his cardinal rule about getting mixed up with any unattached female under the age of eighty.

But she didn't ask. She closed her mouth and handed back his hat. Their hands touched for a moment. The light contact didn't last more than a second, yet Luke's skin tingled from the feel of her soft, exquisitely gentle fingers brushing his. Nothing about this lady was what he expected it to be. He gazed down, reacting to an almost instinctual urge to look into her eyes, to hear her husky voice, to touch her one more time. But she was gone.

Weaving her way through the crowded, closely packed tables, Sarah hoped she could hold off her tears of embarrassment until she was outside the bar. She'd made a first-class fool of herself, and she refused to further humiliate herself by crying in public.

Damn the man. She'd thrown herself on his mercy, and he'd brushed her off like an annoying fly. At least he could have listened to her. Her offer would have been almost as good as Brennermen's, better when he considered that there weren't any religious agendas thrown into the bargain. In court Sarah would have classified Tyrell as a hostile witness. In real life she classified him as a bastard.

Angry tears pricked her eyes. Her vision blurred, she bumped into a table, eliciting several colorful curses from its occupants. She barely heard them. Her mind was jumping ahead to the future and to what she was going to tell the kids. She needed to come up with something, something that would give them hope that everything was going to work out for them. But now even she was having trouble believing that—

A figure loomed in her path. She tried to go around but found that the person moved with her, blocking her way. Looking up, she saw a broad, fleshy face grinning at her with a cruel smile. During her years as a public defender she'd seen much worse, but recently she certainly hadn't.

"What's your hurry, honey?"

Great, Sarah thought. Now she had Godzilla making a pass at her. The end to a perfect day. "Excuse me. I'm trying to get by," she said in her coldest, most intimidating voice.

It didn't faze him. He pressed closer, grasping her forearm in a viselike grip. "Stick around. You and me could have some fun."

"Let me go," she stated, still more annoyed than alarmed. Bullies like this guy fed on terror. The best way to discourage them was with cool, calm indifference.

But her indifference disintegrated as his other arm circled her waist and pulled her hard against his soft, fat stomach. She struggled, only to have his grip tighten around her until she could hardly breathe. Pressed unwillingly against him, she smelled the unwashed odor of his skin and the rancid smell of liquor on his breath as he bent to kiss her.

She looked around for help, but the bar's patrons either ignored her, or backed away into the concealing gloom. Fear mixed with disbelief in her mind. She was being molested, and no one was going to help her. . . .

Suddenly, a figure appeared out of the shadows, a tall, lean man wearing a well-worn Stetson. "The lady asked you to let her go."

Tyrell barely spoke above a whisper, but everyone nearby quieted, frozen by his slow, lethal words. Time stopped. Tension crackled through the air, mounting like static electricity before a lightning strike. Everyone knew an explosion was coming.

Almost everyone. "Back off," the bully said. "Find your own piece of skirt."

"Let her go," Luke repeated, his words dropping like stones through the tension-charged silence. "Let her go, and there won't be any trouble."

Annoyance turned to delight in the larger man's eyes. "Boy, you couldn't be more wrong." He released Sarah so quickly, she nearly lost her balance, then turned his attention to the cowboy.

Luke took a scant second to meet Sarah's eyes and watched as she nodded shakily, indicating that she was all right. Nonetheless, anger rose in Luke. Any man who preyed on defenseless women was pond scum in his view. Balling his hands into fists, he turned toward the bully . . . and ducked just in time to miss the man's swinging arm.

Luke countered with a direct hit to the larger man's midsection. The bully staggered but recovered with alarming speed. Undaunted, Luke delivered a powerful jab to the man's beefy forearm. The big man turned back at him and actually grinned.

"Uh-oh," Luke murmured as he stepped back. He'd given the guy a couple of his best punches, and they hadn't even winded him. Too late he noticed the bully's tree-trunk arms, and the fact that he outweighed Luke by a good hundred pounds. Scum didn't come any bigger, or meaner. And, Luke thought, if he didn't come up with something fast, this big, mean scum was going to wipe the floor with—

"Look out!"

Alerted by Sarah's cry, Luke saw the man's knee come up, headed directly for his groin. He turned, taking the sharp blow on his less vulnerable hip. Even so, pain ripped through his side, doubling him over. His eyes narrowed as he looked up and saw the smug, gloating expression on the bully's face.

Something snapped in Luke. Oblivious to the pain, he reared up and put all his strength into one last punch aimed at wiping away that expression. Luke connected with the man's jaw in a bone-crushing crack, then watched as the bully froze, then toppled to the ground unconscious.

"Serves you right," Luke mumbled, staring at the crumpled figure. He started to turn around, then sucked in his breath as pain shot through his midsection.

Suddenly, Sarah appeared at his side, pulling his arm around her shoulder to help support him. "Nice work, cowboy," she said, easing him toward the door. "Now let's get out of here before one of his buddies tries to make it two out of three."

Sarah turned the steering wheel, heading her truck off the main road and onto the narrow dirt lane that led to her house. The darkness of the spring night closed around her, wrapping her in the sounds and scents that had meant home to her for as long as she could remember. She looked over at her passenger, who was pressed up against the window, sound asleep. His pale hair caught bits of moonlight as she passed in and out of the shadows, but the rest of him remained in unrelenting darkness. Even the hat he clutched so tightly in his lap refused to be defined by the light.

Occasionally Sarah's Irish blood made her fanciful, especially on soft, moonlit nights. And so it seemed to her as if the man at her side had been deserted by the light, and the thought made her sad. Where was his home? she wondered. Did he have sights and smells and dreams to comfort him?

Her thoughts ended abruptly as the front tire caught a pothole. The cab jarred, and her passenger came awake, cursing softly.

"Sorry," she apologized, meaning it. She'd tried to

make the ride as smooth as possible, not an easy thing to do considering the sorry state of most of the roads in this county. She owed him that—and much more. "We'll be at my place in a few minutes."

"I still don't see why I had to come here," he said glumly.

Sarah sighed, tired of responding to this comment. "Look, we've been through this before. That Japanese B-movie monster look-alike almost took you out."

"I'm fine," he stated, but the spasm of pain that crossed his face said otherwise.

"You're not fine, and you know it. If there was a decent hospital within twenty miles, I'd take you in for an X ray. But there isn't, so you'll have to rest up at my place for a few days, until we see if you're really okay."

"I'd rather—"

"I *know* what you'd rather. I just don't happen to care."

He made a deep rasping sound in the back of his throat. At first she thought he was coughing. Then, with a start, she realized he was chuckling.

"Has anyone ever told you how bossy you are?" he asked.

"Only when they're being polite," she replied, grinning.

When she didn't hear him reply, she glanced over at him, wondering if he'd fallen asleep again. He hadn't. Luke sat with his elbow propped on the window, looking out into the night. His chin was slightly raised, as if he were staring at some distant horizon instead of a country lane edged by overgrown trees and bushes. Silver moonlight fell full on his face, illuminating each strong, arrogant feature. Shadows surrounded him, and the backdrop of darkness dramatically sharpened the chiseled lines of his profile.

A curious sadness for him suddenly wound through Sarah. She'd spent plenty of time alone during the past few years—after what her ex-husband had put her through, she wasn't exactly anxious to get back into a relationship—but she'd always had friends and family to ease her loneliness. But this man seemed entirely solitary, as remote as the stars that glittered in the night sky above. Remote and brilliantly, bitterly cold.

He was, she thought objectively, one of the most handsome men she'd ever seen. The poor lighting in the bar had hidden the details of his appearance from her. She'd only noticed that he was tall, lean, and had a disposition more stubborn than hers, which took some doing. After the fight she'd been too busy arguing him into her truck to notice what he looked like.

She noticed now. He was absolutely gorgeous, a blond Adonis with a healthy portion of Clint Eastwood thrown in for good measure. He was the kind of man who could seduce a woman by just raising his eyebrow. He had *great* eyebrows. Eyebrows, and—

Sarah, you're losing it! she admonished herself. She dragged her gaze away from his chiseled features, belatedly realizing that inviting a drop-dead hunk into her home wasn't the wisest of moves. After all, it was six months since she'd had her last date. And it was a great deal longer than that since she'd . . . well, since she'd had—

"Nice place you've got here," Luke said suddenly.

His words jarred her back to reality. "Uh, thanks," she replied, hoping he didn't notice her breathlessness.

Apparently, he didn't. "Lots of space," he continued, still gazing out the window. "Level ground, fertile . . . what's your cash crop?"

"Weeds, mostly," she said, her worries overriding her embarrassment. She'd poured over her agricultural textbooks, but so far she hadn't put the theories into practice. The stink Brennermen and some of her other neighbors had kicked up over her children had eaten up all her time and energy, putting her even further behind schedule. With spring nearly half over she knew she'd have to make a decision soon or lose the better part of the growing season. Maybe that's what Brennermen was counting on. . . .

"You mean you don't grow anything?" Luke said, sounding appalled at the waste of good land.

"Well, we have a vegetable garden. I laid it out, but the kids are the ones doing all the work."

"Kids? You've got *kids*?"

"Well, yes," said Sarah, wondering why he sounded so surprised.

"But . . . you said you weren't married."

"I'm not. These days you don't have to be married to have kids."

Even the darkness couldn't disguise the startled look on his face. Great, she thought. First he thinks I'm a prostitute, now he thinks I'm an unwed mother. She opened her mouth to explain, but he spoke first.

"Look, I might as well tell you up front. I don't much like kids."

His tone implied that he equated kids with natural disasters, nuclear holocausts, and heaven only knew what else. Well, she reasoned, at least he was honest about it. Most of the single men she knew felt the same way, but they refused to admit it. They used all sorts of excuses to cover up their dislike. "I'm not a good role model," one had told her. "I can't give them the quality time they need," another had said. The worst excuse came from a philosophy professor she'd dated, who'd informed her that his "aura was all wrong for parental nurturing."

Few of them understood why she'd left a prestigious, profitable career as a defense attorney in Dallas and taken up residence on a run-down farm smack in the middle of nowhere, East Texas. None of them understood the passion that drove her, why she *had* to do what she was doing. Not that she really expected them to. Hell, even her parents thought she was crazy.

If Luke Tyrell knew her background, he, too, certainly would think she was crazy. She sighed, worn down from battles that had nothing to do with him.

"Don't worry, cowboy. With that effervescent personality of yours, my kids probably won't like you much either."

"Effervescent?"

"Yeah. It means—"

"I know what it means. I've just never been compared to an antacid tablet before."

They were driving through a patch of deep shadow. The darkness might have hidden the smile on his lips, but it couldn't mask the amusement in his voice. Gorgeous *and* a sense of humor, Sarah amended morosely. Not to mention the fact that he'd risked his neck to save her from Godzilla's beefy clutches. All at once the cab seemed awfully small and entirely too intimate for her peace of mind. She could hear him breathing; she could smell his heady scent mixing with the wool of his sheepskin jacket. So masculine. She wondered if he listened to her breathing, which was becoming more erratic by the minute.

Luckily, they were almost home. Sarah swung her truck past the rail fence that bounded her front yard and into the driveway of the Corners. The main house loomed ahead, frosted with moonlight, built with the rambling magnificence of a bygone age. Her first memories had been of this house and the summers she'd spent here with her aunt Connie. Even then the structure had been falling into genteel disrepair, but she'd been too young to see it. Now even the darkness couldn't hide the missing roof shingles, the busted trellis, the broken porch slats. Loving the place as she did, she felt each deficiency as a physical wound. An injury to an old friend . . .

"That's why they won't help you, isn't it?"

"Who?" she asked.

"The townspeople. In the bar you told me they wouldn't help you. It's because of your kids, and the fact that you're not married. Right?"

Sarah pulled her truck to a stop. "Not exactly."

Luke didn't seem to hear her. "Damn," he continued, pounding his fist against the dashboard for emphasis. "Those sanctimonious hypocrites. They talk about God and the Bible, but when someone really needs help . . ." His words dwindled away as he shook his head in disgust. "Look, Miss Gallagher, I don't mean to pry, but couldn't the kids' father take some responsibility? Couldn't he help you out?"

Plan C, Sarah thought as she recalled the detailed scenarios she'd mapped out to save her place. Like so many of the others, it hadn't washed. "It wouldn't be practical. I mean, none of them lives in this area—"

"Them!" Luke's jaw dropped to his boots. "You mean there's more than *one*?"

Seeing the complete shock on his face, Sarah let her mischievous nature got the better of her. "Six, actually. Or is it seven? One tends to lose track after a while."

"Lose track?" he repeated, his jaw dropping farther.

Sarah couldn't contain her laughter any longer. It bubbled up inside her like a refreshing spring, making her realize how long it had been since she'd felt this lighthearted. But almost immediately she felt guilty. She owed the man too much to laugh at his expense, even if he did look so comically shocked by her apparent lack of morals. "I'm sorry," she said, placing her hand apologetically on his arm. "I should have explained about my children before. They're—"

But before she could finish her sentence, the front door opened, throwing a stream of yellow light across the yard. "Hey, she's home," yelled a voice, young and full of joy. "Sarah's home!"

Other voices joined in as the children poured through the doorway, welcoming Sarah with a rollicking chorus of greetings and questions, and a few pointed comments about how some of them had misbehaved while she was gone. Barking dogs added to the general melee. One of them jumped up to the passenger window and thrusted his wet nose over it toward the startled occupant. Luke drew back, glancing at Sarah with an expression close to horror on his face. "Damn, woman, how many kids have you got?"

TWO

She had five kids. Or at least, that's how many bodies Luke counted circling around him as he stood in the front hall. Because of their constant motion he got only the vaguest impression of each of them—a brown-haired boy with thick, owl-eyed glasses, a small blond girl clutching a dog-eared teddy bear, a tall, dark-haired youth with cold eyes, a thin, redheaded girl with freckles on her nose, and a quiet girl who seemed older yet more fragile than the rest.

They fired questions at him with the speed of a machine gun, while their openly curious gazes bored into him, disturbing old memories and old pains. Hell, he'd rather face five barroom bullies—five times five—than five kids.

Sarah did her best to quiet them. "Mr. Tyrell can't answer all your questions now. He's been hurt."

"Is he bleeding?" the boy with glasses asked eagerly. "I know what to do if he's bleeding."

"He is *not* bleeding, Micah," Sarah said, trying to maintain order. She loved her children, but even she had to admit their manners could stand some improvement. "He was in a fight."

"A fight?" scoffed the dark-haired youth. "Doesn't look like it was much of a fight."

The red-haired girl spoke up. "That's because you always leave fights looking like a truck ran over you."

"Yeah, Spots, well, at least I don't have a face someone could play connect the dots with."

"At least I'm not too stupid to live, you—" She finished the sentence with a word that blistered even Luke's seasoned ears.

"Jenny!" Sarah cried, appalled. She gave Luke a glance that somehow managed to be apologetic and defensive at once, then turned back to the red-haired girl. "Jenny, please, we have a guest."

Jenny, alias Spots, merely shrugged. "So?"

"So we don't use that kind of language around guests," Sarah explained patiently. "We actually don't use that kind of language at all."

The dark-haired boy laughed. "Yeah, Spots. Even I know that."

"Well, it's probably the only thing you do know," Jenny fired back.

"Says who?"

"Says me, you son of a—"

"Quiet!" Luke roared.

The whole room fell silent—even the dogs stopped barking. About time, Luke thought. This incessant arguing was making his head hurt, which was making his side hurt, which was bringing his already heated temper to a boil. Kids in general irritated him, but this gang of juvenile delinquents in training threatened to drive him crazy.

"Look," he said through clenched teeth, "I don't care if you use the foulest language on earth. All I want is a bed for the night and a little peace and quiet to go with it. So if you don't mind—"

Luke stopped as he felt a tug on his sleeve. He looked down and saw the blond girl with the teddy bear standing by his elbow. "You're pretty," she said, smiling up at him with wide, trusting eyes. "I'm going to keep you."

"You're what?" he said, his words strangled by confusion.

Sarah reached out her hand and gently drew the girl from his side. "Valerie, honey, you know we've talked about this before. You can't keep people the way you keep your stuffed animals. Besides," she said, her mouth turning up in a loving smile, "you wouldn't want Mr. Bear to get jealous, would you?"

"No," Valerie agreed, hugging her tattered teddy bear to her chest. She gave Luke a soberly appraising look. "But I think Mr. Bear wants to keep him too."

Luke kept his mouth shut. He'd dealt with all kinds in his life—drunks, thieves, people who'd cut you for a dollar and not think twice about it. He had a reputation for meeting trouble head-on and never backing down from a fight, even when he knew the odds were against him. But he'd never faced the kind of trouble he saw in this little girl's eyes. Soft and trusting, they reached in and touched the deepest part of him. The part that still hurt, even after all these years.

Luke couldn't stand to look into those eyes anymore. He turned away quickly, too quickly for his wounded body's comfort. Pain blossomed through him, and he winced, stumbling against the wall for support.

"Luke!" Sarah cried, immediately at his side.

"I'm . . . fine."

"Like hell you are. You're white as a sheet," she said, moving to his side and propping his weight against her. She spoke over her shoulder to the children, delivering orders with the ease of a four-star general. "Rafe, you and Jenny get the first-aid kit and bring it to the den. Micah, you get the dogs out of here. And, Lyn," she said, speaking to the silent blonde, "see that Val and Mr. Bear get to bed on time."

The children nodded almost in unison and set about their tasks without a word of protest. Luke watched them scatter, amazed that anyone could whip those little hell-raisers into line. "Well, I'll be damned," he murmured.

"Probably," Sarah agreed, as she started to help him down the hallway. "But first we're going to see to that side of yours."

It wasn't easy getting to the den. Even with Sarah's assistance, pain sprinted across Luke's side every time he took a step. Still, he had to admit the experience had its good points. Sarah's body was pressed against his, giving him a chance to find out what kind of shape she was hiding under her baggy shirt and padded vest. He'd expected her to be thin and scrawny, with sharp angles to match her sharp personality. Instead, he discovered a body that was soft and enticingly rounded, with curves that would have given a beauty queen a run for her money. Underneath her oversized clothes Sarah was 100 percent female, and Luke's reaction to her, despite the blow to his side, was definitely 100 percent male. Well, he reasoned, there was nothing wrong with a little healthy lust, as long as he didn't let it get out of hand.

That sentiment, however, proved to be easier said than done. Sarah led him through the oak doors of the den and settled him on the large, overstuffed couch. She stood in front of him, hands propped on her waist, and said evenly, "Take off your shirt."

Luke looked up sharply in surprise. "What?"

Husky laughter met his startled gaze. "Don't worry, cowboy. I only want to get a look at that side of yours. See if you've broken any ribs."

"I haven't," he said curtly. Her deep, throaty laughter grated his nerves like sandpaper. "I can take care of myself."

"Right. And what are you going to use to check your back? The eyes in the back of your head?" She crossed her arms in front of her, a no-nonsense smile on her lips. "Now take off your shirt . . . unless you want me to call Micah in to do it for you."

Luke recalled the boy with glasses who'd been so interested in his injury. "You mean the kid who was half-hoping I was bleeding to death?"

"He was not," Sarah said defensively. "Micah's just inquisitive. He wants to be a doctor someday."

"God help his patients," Luke commented dryly. He glanced at Sarah and caught the emerald gleam in her eye, a spark of humor and challenge. The room's single light, a squat, jade-colored table lamp with a red fringed shade, cast a ruby light on her face. The red glow gave a warmth to her soft skin and picked up the auburn highlights in her dark chestnut hair. Yet neither the flush of her skin nor the burnished sparks in her hair matched the intriguing defiance that sparkled in her green eyes.

Once again Luke experienced that uncanny recognition, as if he were seeing part of himself reflected in her eyes. Shaken, he looked down and began to unbutton his cotton shirt. "How'd you get saddled with that boy, anyway?"

" 'That boy' is named Micah. And I didn't 'get saddled' with him," she protested. "I chose Micah specially, as I chose each one of my children."

Luke chuckled humorlessly. "Lady, no offense," he said as he finished unbuttoning his shirt and began to slip it off his shoulders, "but you need to get your eyes examined. Maybe your head, too, since no one in her right mind would choose to be in the same room with those delinquents, much less want to adopt them."

"They're not delinquents!" she said, the spark in her eyes turning to fire. "You're as bad as everyone else—judging without proof. It's not fair. Honestly, even criminals are innocent until proven—"

A sharp intake in breath stopped her tirade. Luke raised his head at the sudden silence and saw that her gaze was riveted to his now-exposed side.

Luke looked down and saw an ugly bruise just south of his rib cage. Hard experience had taught him a bruise like this would clear up in a few days, though it would hurt like hell while it healed. "It's not so bad."

"Not bad?" she said as she knelt down to get a closer look. "Lord, man, it's the size of Dallas. It must hurt like crazy."

Crazy didn't begin to cover it. The returning sensation made his side ache with pure fire. But for some unfathomable reason he didn't want her to know. He shrugged his shoulders nonchalantly, ignoring the fact that the slight gesture sent pain shooting through layers of tortured muscles. "I've had worse."

"Liar," she commented, though somehow the word held no condemnation. She reached out tentatively and pressed her fingers gently against his skin. "I don't think you've got any broken ribs, but maybe we ought to get you X-rayed to be sure. What do you think?"

At that moment thinking wasn't high on Luke's list of priorities. He was too busy concentrating on the way Sarah's light touch felt against his hot, aching skin. Her fingers whispered over him, delicate as a butterfly's wing, yet the pain quieted wherever she touched. How long had it been since a woman touched him like this, as if she truly cared?

Soothing peace flowed through him, lulling his senses. Sighing, he glanced down and took pleasure in watching the lamplight pick out the shifting auburn highlights in her thick, unruly hair. A man could get lost in hair like that. As he watched, she pushed a strand off her forehead, tucking it behind one of her ears. Ears had never interested Luke before—he tended to focus on the more basic parts of a woman's anatomy—but Sarah's fascinated him. Shell-perfect, the delicate folds of her ear begged to be caressed, to be kissed, tasted, devoured.

Luke cleared his throat. "Aren't you finished yet?" he asked gruffly.

She continued her examination as if he hadn't spoken.

Her touch did things to his insides, things that had nothing to do with his wound. Good Lord, couldn't this woman tell what torture she was putting him through? "I said—"

"I heard you," she said without bothering to look up. "Geez, you're such a grouch. Anyone ever tell you that?"

"Only when they're being polite."

She looked up then, her mouth curved in the same sweet, mischievous smile that he'd first glimpsed back at the bar—the smile that had set warning bells ringing in his mind. He listened for those bells now, but the damn things didn't sound a peep, deserting him in his hour of need. Her grin was as intoxicating as her touch, and he felt his own stern lips curve into an answering smile.

"There, you're smiling," she said, honestly pleased. "That's better."

"Is it?" he asked. He bent closer until his quickening breath stirred the curling tendrils of her hair. His voice grew soft, husky with unmistakable desire. "Is it really?"

Her smile died. He watched as awareness dawned in her eyes, awareness that she was fingering the torso of a half-naked man whose mouth was within kissing distance of her own. Gruffness had failed to ruffle the surface of her cool exterior, but embarrassment succeeded.

She drew away, standing well out of his reach. Once again she clasped her arms in front of her, but this time the gesture seemed more nervous than defiant. "I'd . . . better go . . . to see what happened to the kids. Rafe and Jenny should have been here by now."

They've probably killed each other, Luke thought, remembering the barbs the two had traded earlier. He should get angry or something, he thought, to take the edge off the smoldering fire she'd unwittingly kindled inside him. He watched Sarah walk to the door. She seemed prepared to slip out as quickly and completely as she had in the murky bar. That time her leaving had struck Luke with a sudden, inexplicable sense of loss. This time was no different, except that the feeling was ten times stronger. "Wait."

The sudden request appeared to surprise her almost as much as it did him. She paused, her hand resting on the doorframe as she hesitantly looked back at him. "Why?"

Good question, he thought. Unfortunately, he didn't have a good answer. "You . . . you never told me why you adopted these, uh, little angels. Most people would have taken one look at them and run in the opposite direction."

The glow of the lamp was too dim to reach her face, but the lack of light couldn't hide the smile in her voice. "That's exactly why I adopted them," she said, and left without another word.

That cinched it, he thought, as he raked his fingers through his hair in frustration. The lady was nuts. Certifiable. But then, he should have figured that out from the start, when she'd walked into a seedy bar, unescorted, and practically propositioned him. A sane woman just didn't come on to a man that way. But then, a sane man didn't tackle a barroom rowdy twice his size, especially over a woman he barely knew. A crazy woman he barely knew, he amended.

Yet he had defended her, rushing to her rescue like some white knight. And gotten the tar beat out of him in the process. He asked himself why. She was good-looking—no, better than good-looking. She had a dynamite body and emerald eyes that could haunt a man's dreams, not to mention those really amazing ears. But the more Luke focused on her attributes, the more he realized it wasn't only physical attraction operating here. She'd stirred feelings inside him he thought he had laid to rest years ago, feelings of tenderness, protection, and trust. She made him remember the kind of man he'd wanted to be, the kind of man he'd been until . . .

"Damn!" he muttered, fighting the memories. He followed the word with a string of profanities. It didn't help. Frustrated, he grabbed his shirt and rose from the couch, shoving his arms roughly into the sleeves. The movement hurt, but he welcomed the pain. It cleared his mind and reminded him that women and trouble went hand in hand. Luke Tyrell, of all people, had reason to remember that particular lesson. After all, he'd had one hell of a teacher—

"Mister?"

Startled, Luke spun around, his muscles taut and ready for action. His well-honed instincts had saved him more than once, but in this case they weren't needed. The speaker was the little blond-haired girl, the youngest of Sarah's "angels." She stood in the doorway, clutching her teddy bear to her chest, and stared at him with her unnervingly innocent eyes.

Hell, this was the last thing he needed. "Go away, little girl," he said, straightening slowly from his fighting stance. He lifted his hand and waved her away. "Er, shoo."

She didn't budge. "Do you feel bad?"

Bad? He felt as if he'd been bucked off four horses all at once. His unplanned combat maneuver had pulled every muscle in his body, even some he didn't know he had. "Yeah," he said, trying to keep from wincing at the new pain. "Yeah, kid. I feel plenty bad."

The girl nodded. Luke expected her to leave, but she didn't. Instead, she took a cautious step closer. "Sometimes Mr. Bear makes me feel better," she said, lifting her stuffed animal up to him. "You can hold him if you want to."

Luke stared down at the bear and the girl, but he didn't see them. He saw another child holding another toy. Another life. Deep inside him old wounds throbbed to life, ones that time had dulled but never healed. His physical agony was nothing compared to it. Less than nothing. He felt dead, frozen, and when he spoke, his words were barely audible. "Get out, kid."

"But, Mr. Bear—"

"I don't give a damn about your bear!" he said, his voice rising. Years of suppressed anger poured out of him in a rush. "Get out! Now!"

The girl's arm dropped like a stone. Her lower lip quivered, and her eyes filled with tears of fright. Too late Luke realized he'd taken out his pent-up rage on an innocent child. He was a hard man but not a cruel one, and he was genuinely disgusted by what he'd done. He reached down to comfort her, but she shied away, moving with the speed of a seasoned prizefighter. That kind of agility only came with practice. Sweet Lord.

"Don't touch her!"

Luke looked up and saw Sarah rushing into the room, her arms loaded down with a stack of blankets and pillows with a medical kit balanced precariously on the top. The whole lot of it crashed unheeded to the floor as she knelt down and gathered the frightened girl into her arms. She murmured soothing words of comfort to her child, then turned a gaze of pure fury on Luke. "How could you? Valerie's father abused her. She's just beginning to recover."

"I'm sorry. I didn't know."

"As if you care," Sarah said, tightening her grip on the girl. "You've made it very clear that you don't like children."

Luke winced. "That doesn't mean I go around yelling at them."

"You just did!"

They glared at each other in tense silence, neither willing to give an inch. Finally, Sarah said, "I invited you here, so you can stay the night. But tomorrow morning, bruise or no bruise, I want you to leave."

"That suits me fine," Luke agreed, his mouth pulling into a hard line. "I'm not about to spend another night in this . . . asylum. No wonder they want to close you down."

She went still as stone. Luke spotted the bright sheen of tears in her eyes and knew he'd hurt her deeply. Instantly contrite, he reached out to her, wishing he could wrap her in his arms and make her forget his angry words. He never got the chance. Sarah shied away from him as her daughter had, and headed for the door.

At the last moment she stopped and turned back to him. "I should have left you at the bar," she said, her words coolly precise. "You and that bully are two of a kind."

Luke met her gaze squarely. He wanted like hell to contradict her, but he couldn't. For reasons she couldn't begin to understand, he knew she was absolutely right.

Long after Valerie had fallen asleep in her arms, Sarah stared up at her bedroom ceiling, listening to the sounds of the night, trying to take solace in their familiarity. She found none. Her anger had long since subsided into intellectual examination—the result of her disposition and her years of legal training. But the more she considered what had happened this evening, the more confused she became. And that confusion rested squarely on the broad shoulders of Luke Tyrell.

What was it about that man? He'd yelled at one of her kids, a crime only slightly less damning than mass murder in her eyes. Valerie and the others had been through so much in their short lives. They didn't need a sarcastic, mean-spirited cowboy to add to their disillusionment and fear. Yet Sarah couldn't help feeling there was more to Luke's anger than mere child dislike. The same instinct that had made her the nightmare of every D.A. in the city told her Luke hadn't been angry with Valerie, but with someone or something else. It didn't excuse his behavior, but it explained it. It also added to her confusion.

What in his past had made him so angry? And more to the point, why should she care? By tomorrow he'd be out of her life. By the day after she'd have forgotten all about him—his bold eyes, his rock-solid muscles, his maddeningly masculine scent . . .

Groaning, she turned over on her stomach and buried her head in her pillow. Damn the man for being so sexy. And damn her for noticing. Mothers should be immune to these sort of feelings. It wasn't fair.

Fair is where you take your hog to win blue ribbons. . . .

Sarah smiled as her great-aunt's words came back to her. Aunt Connie. Simply remembering the tough-minded, tender-hearted old woman made her feel warm and safe inside. Connie had been one of the original independent women, a widow who chose to run her farm by herself rather than sell it and retreat to a more socially acceptable life in town. In the end she'd passed it on to another independent woman, leaving Sarah the Corners in her will when she'd died two years before. "Don't just follow your dream," she'd written in a letter enclosed with the deed. "Run after it full tilt and grab it."

Sarah had followed her aunt's advice. She'd grabbed her dream with both hands, turning the Corners into a home for kids that the rest of the world had forgotten or simply didn't want. When people told her she was crazy, she took comfort in the fact that they'd said the same thing about Aunt Connie.

Did Luke think she was crazy? Probably, she thought, considering he'd used the word "asylum." She hated to admit how much his use of the word had hurt her. But it wasn't crazy to love someone. And it wasn't crazy to try to build a decent home for these wonderful kids, even if she did stir up every right-wing fundamentalist from East Texas to Louisiana.

Eventually, Sarah fell asleep, enjoying a deep, dreamless sleep until the alarm clock's unpleasant buzz startled her awake. Not a morning person, Sarah was about to growl an equally unpleasant word in response but stifled it when she realized Valerie was still beside her. Her eyes winking open momentarily, the child yawned and turned over and was sound asleep again before her blond head hit the pillow. Valerie could sleep through a train wreck.

Smiling with a mixture of love and envy, Sarah leaned over and kissed her daughter lightly on the cheek. Then she swung her legs over the side of the bed. She paused at the window to drink in the fresh morning breeze, heavy with promise for the coming day. Outside she saw the animals beginning to stir. The chickens began their choppy bowing and prancing around the yard, as if paying homage to the rooster who sat on the fence post, red-combed and silent, as usual, at the start of the new day. Cogburn's arbitrary nature had almost landed him in the stewpot, but Sarah had rescued him, as she'd done with so many of the other animals on the farm.

Turning, she caught sight of the clock and almost choked at how late it was. She rushed to her closet and threw on a pair of worn jeans and a faded T-shirt from a rock concert of a group that had disbanded years ago. Her clothes were clean and comfortable, her only requirements for her wardrobe these days. She fought a comb through her thick curls, vowing, as she did every morning, to cut her hair before the week was out. Then she slipped into a pair of scuffed loafers and headed out of her room. She was down the curved stairway and in the front hall before she remembered about Luke.

Oh Lord, she thought, veering to the den. Luke Tyrell was the last person she needed to be worrying about this morning. She was already running late, and her good-hearted children were probably well on their way to destroying the kitchen—the Valdez oil slick was easier to clean up than Micah's "super-special pancake batter." But she had to warn Luke to stay out of sight until the feeding frenzy was over and her kids were safely on their way to school. Then she would take him back to Bubba's parking lot and his truck, so that he could get on with his life, and she could get on with hers.

She reached the den and knocked on the door. She heard a muffled response, which she took to be a "come in." She put her hand on the brass knob, turned it, and pushed open the heavy door.

Immediately, she realized she'd made a mistake. Luke hadn't told her to come in. He couldn't. He was asleep on the couch, sprawled across the overstuffed piece of furniture like a rag doll. Even as she watched, he shook his head slightly, mumbling something in his sleep. That's what I heard, she thought, and turned to leave.

Luke's voice called her back. "Annie," he murmured.

Sarah paused, her curiosity piqued. Who, she wondered, was Annie? Was it his sister, his lover?

"Annie, where are you?"

Sarah's heart constricted in her chest. She'd never heard anyone sound so lost, so lonely. She tiptoed across the carpet, stepping through the pieces of morning light that dappled the floor. But the light didn't reach Luke's couch. Darkness surrounded him, accenting the deeply etched lines of his troubled, tortured expression. "Annie . . ."

"I'm here," Sarah whispered, hoping it was the right thing to say. "I'm right here."

Apparently, it was. The worry lines eased a bit, and his breathing became deeper. "I love you."

Tears pricked Sarah's eyes. She turned away, then slowly turned back. Asleep, he looked impossibly young and touchingly vulnerable. She reached out and gently smoothed a lock of hair away from his forehead. "I love you too," she whispered. "Go back to sleep."

A minute later she was heading to the kitchen, trying vainly to put Luke and his dreams of his lover out of her mind. She'd wanted only to help him, but she feared that instead she had trespassed, stepping into his dreams with the muddy boots of her good intentions. She felt like a voyeur, peeping through a keyhole at another man's life. "I love you," he'd said. The words had been meant for Annie, but it was Sarah who heard them and Sarah who cried.

Sarah had little time to ponder her feelings, because she heard angry voices coming from the kitchen. She assumed Rafe and Jenny were at it again until she got closer and realized that at least one of the voices belonged to an adult. Running now, she crossed the formal dining room and shoved open the swinging door. Her children were ranged along one side of the large central table, glaring at the man who stood inside the back door, his wide, dark shape blocking the morning light.

Brennermen.

THREE

I love you.

The words echoed through Luke's mind long after the dream images had shimmered away. He opened his eyes slowly, blinking at the light that filled the room. Luke always slept with the curtains drawn and the shades pulled down, closing himself in the isolation of his rented accommodations. Privacy was one of the few things he valued that money *could* buy. But this morning sunlight poured through his open window, bringing with it the rich scent of spring blossoms and the sweet, lilting song of a distant mockingbird. He turned, catching sight of the long, elegant windows and the elaborate green velvet curtains that belonged to another era. Holiday Inns sure have changed, he thought groggily.

Then he remembered this wasn't his room, that this wasn't even a motel.

Yawning, he rubbed the sleep from his eyes. His

palm brushed the rough stubble on his chin, and he muttered a curse as he recalled that he'd left his shaving kit sitting in the back of his truck in Bubba's parking lot. Memories came together in a rush, reminding him of the fight, the kids, Sarah. . . .

I love you, whispered the voice in his mind.

Luke eased himself to a sitting position, cautiously testing his muscles. He stretched one long limb after the other and was pleasantly surprised to discover he'd lost most of last night's soreness. And his bruise—at least the part of it he could see—had grown noticeably smaller. He felt incredibly good considering the blows and punches. And miraculously good since he'd just woken up from another dream about Annie.

The dreams had haunted him for years. The memories he'd spent his days not remembering came on with a vengeance at night. Usually, he awoke in a pool of sweat, filled with a black paralyzing pain that lasted several days and took several bottles of whiskey to numb. The few people he knew well had learned to avoid him during these spells, and the ones who didn't often lived to regret it. More than once he'd woken up in the local jail, facing a charge of drunk and disorderly.

But this time the dream had been different. This time it had ended in hope, not bleak despair. "I love you," Annie had said. But though Annie's image had spoken the words, the voice he'd heard had been Sarah's.

"This squirrelly household is making *me* crazy,"

Luke grumbled. Kids, dogs, and Lord only knew what else lived in this nutty place. He shoved his arms into the sleeves of his shirt, leaned down, and tugged on the black leather boots he'd set beside the couch the night before. They molded to his muscular calves like a second skin, but he frowned as he noticed how scuffed and worn they were. He frowned even more deeply when he realized *why* he was noticing. The last thing he needed was to care about what a certain woman thought about his boots, especially since that woman had the sharpest tongue and the quickest temper this side of Galveston. And a touch that could take a man to heaven without half trying.

He shook his head, trying, with limited success, to shake out the memory too. Failing that, he reached for his final piece of clothing—his hat. It wasn't there. He started to search the room for it, then remembered he'd left it with his coat on the side table in the entry hall.

Damn! He rubbed his chin in frustration. He'd spent years training that Stetson to fit his head, to get its brim to slope to the exact angle to shade his eyes without hampering his vision. His hat was the closest thing he had to an old friend, and those kids better not have messed with it.

He strode to the doors and pushed them open, entering a hall. Sunlight dappled the walls and spilled bright rivers across the wide, varnished floors. Luke barely noticed. He turned his head left, then right, wondering which direction would lead him back to the front door. He tried to recall how Sarah had brought him to the den last night, but his memory was muddled by pain and carnal desire for his hostess's body. Served him right, he thought ruefully. That's what he got for lusting after a harebrained woman.

He still felt her fingers against his naked skin, her butterfly touch stroking magic through his body. Physical awareness he could handle, but she'd moved him in a deeper, more essential way. She'd rocked his foundations and disturbed the sleeping dragons in his soul, his buried memories. *I love you. . . .*

"I don't need this," he muttered. Tired of indecision, he turned left and walked down the hall with long, confident strides. Within minutes he was lost. The hallway twisted and turned on itself, and every step led him deeper into the maze.

He turned a corner and saw something that convinced him he'd come the wrong way. Directly ahead was a foot-wide hole in the wall, a jagged opening that revealed brick and pipe. Even distracted by pain and lust, he couldn't have missed something that size. Curious, he examined the opening, noting that it was an amateur job but a good one. And a lucky one, too, considering the hole just missed the main support by a couple of inches.

Luke had no doubt that Sarah not only had wielded the sledgehammer but enjoyed doing it. Apparently, her talents weren't limited to accosting strange cowboys in seedy bars and collecting unwanted kids. In his mind's eye he envisioned her with her chestnut hair flying as she blithely knocked out pieces of the wall. Most women wouldn't have dared pick up a hammer, much less attempt to take down a wall, but Sarah wasn't most women. "She's a menace," he said, shaking his head. But he couldn't quite keep the corners of his mouth from creeping up into a smile.

Voices jarred him from his musings. Finally, he thought as he hurried toward the sound, a way out of this labyrinth! Turning a corner, he entered the dining room, a magnificently outdated room with a crystal chandelier hanging over a huge mahogany table. Except for the opulent furnishings the room was empty—and quiet. Luke wondered if he'd taken yet another wrong turn. He was about to retrace his steps when he heard an angry voice coming from the other side of the closed kitchen door.

"For the last time—Corners is not for sale."

It was Sarah, and from the sound of her voice she was fit to be tied. Good Lord, he wondered, grimacing, didn't that woman ever let up?

Luke couldn't hear much of the reply, only that it came from a man. Poor guy, he thought. He rubbed his bristled cheek. If he'd had a shave, a shower, and a decent cup of coffee, he'd have gone in and helped the man defend himself. But as things stood, he wasn't up to facing Miss Gallagher's formidable wrath.

"I don't care if you offer me a million dollars, Brennermen. You can't force us out!"

Brennermen. Luke forgot about showers, shaves, and other personal comforts. He crossed the room, his long legs making short work of the distance, and pushed the door open a crack. Sarah was standing with her back to the tiled kitchen counter, her arms protectively circling Valerie and the red-haired girl, Jenny. The older girl and the dark-haired boy stood nearby, while bespectacled Micah sat at the kitchen table, his cereal spoon poised as if for attack. They were, Luke decided, the sorriest bunch of fighters he'd ever seen. Still, he had to admire the way the mismatched group closed ranks in a battle.

Brennermen spoke, his voice smooth and beguiling. "You misjudge me. I'm not trying to force anyone out. It's the building inspector—"

"Who happens to be your brother-in-law," Sarah fired back.

Luke grinned, impressed in spite of himself by her rapid-fire style. She might be crazy as a hoot owl, but she was damn magnificent in a fight. Standing arrow-straight, her chin held high, she looked ready to take on the whole world for her children. She had the courage of ten men, but Luke knew it took more than courage to win a battle.

He pushed the door open a little wider until he could see Brennermen's profile. Well-groomed and confident, the older man looked only mildly perturbed by Sarah's opposition. Brennermen clearly was used to having things done his way and didn't like being crossed.

Luke felt suddenly and inexplicably protective of Sarah and her brood. What was the matter with him?

Keeping out of other people's business was his cardinal rule. This wasn't his fight, he reminded himself. But he stayed by the door and listened just the same.

"Nevertheless, it's the law," Brennermen said, his smug expression showing no trace of concern. "You wouldn't want to go against the law, would you?"

Sarah's jaw tightened. "I *know* the law. I also know that half the houses in this county don't meet the required standards. Why don't you inspect some of them?"

Jenny piped up. "Yeah, why don't you inspect some of them, you—"

Jenny's colorful expletive momentarily shocked the righteous smile from Brennermen's face. Instead of correcting Jenny as she usually did, Luke saw Sarah's hard, determined mouth turn up in the faintest hint of a grin. Damn, he thought, I could get to like this woman.

But Sarah's victory was small and short-lived.

"You can't argue your way out of this one," Brennermen said, his voice hard and heavy as a judge's gavel. "In sixty days your home is going to be inspected, like it or not. And you and I both know that you haven't got a snowball's chance in hell of passing it. Face facts, Miss Gallagher. Sell out now while you still can."

The room was deathly quiet. All eyes turned to Sarah. She still held her chin high, but her face had lost nearly all of its color. Luke guessed that her courage was flagging. His hands balled into tight fists.

For the past ten years he'd made a habit of walking away from trouble, but this time he simply couldn't step aside, even though the last thing he needed was to spend the next two months doing hard labor for short wages. A smart man would shut the door and walk away, leaving Sarah and her kids to their fate.

But smart didn't seem to matter much where this woman was concerned. Luke knew he could no more walk away than he could have left her to fend for herself against the bully the night before. For reasons he couldn't understand—reasons he didn't want to understand—he had to help her. "Hell, I *must* be out of my mind." He pushed open the door and entered the kitchen.

The quiet room exploded into sound. "Mr. Tyrell!" the children cried, all in different tones and different levels of surprise. Sarah's eyes grew wide as she mouthed his name, but no sound came from her lips. Those damn lips, Luke thought, dragging his gaze away. He wasn't sure if the expression on her face was heartfelt relief or appalled surprise. He hated himself for wondering.

Ignoring the stir he caused, Luke sauntered over to the coffeepot. " 'Morning, Miss Gallagher. Kids." He paused, waiting a full breath before adding, "Brennermen."

The older man's brows shot up. He looked even more astonished than Sarah. "What are you doing here?"

Luke poured himself a mug of coffee and took an

unhurried sip before answering. "At the moment I'm enjoying a cup of Miss Gallagher's fine Java."

"That's not what I meant," Brennermen barked. "You told me you were on your way to Houston to take a job on an oil rig."

"I was," Luke said truthfully. He took another sip, using the moment to catch Sarah's gaze. "But a man can change his mind, can't he?"

He watched her eyes widen almost imperceptibly. She was good at hiding her emotions—too good. People didn't learn that talent by chance, and usually the lessons were far from pleasant. What trouble, he wondered, had taught her how to shut herself up like that? *What mysteries hid beneath the surface of those beautiful emerald eyes?*

"Good Lord, Sarah," Brennermen said, "don't tell me you've hired this man?"

His tone made it sound like a mortal sin. "Why not?" she countered. "You offered him a job."

"That's different. I'm not a divorced woman living on an isolated farm. Tyrell's got a reputation for trouble that spans three states. For trouble and . . . other things," he said, glancing meaningfully first at Luke, then at her. "People will talk."

"Really? Well, let them," Sarah said. "Those people, those good Christian people—you included—haven't lifted a finger to help me or my family since we came here."

"I, er—that's not true," Brennermen sputtered.

Sarah closed the distance between them until she

was standing nose-to-breastbone in front of the man. "The hell it isn't. Whatever Mr. Tyrell's past, he's been more of a friend to me in the last twenty-four hours than this whole town has in all the time we've lived here."

Luke's coffee cup stilled halfway to his lips. Friend? He hadn't been anyone's friend for a long, long time. He didn't want to be. He was a loner and liked it that way. It was how he survived.

Lowering his coffee cup, he glanced at Sarah, surprised and a little annoyed by her choice of words. He sought out her gaze, determined to give her a quelling stare before she could make any more unjustified statements.

And time stopped. Anger had stripped away the gem-hard surface of her eyes, and he caught a glimpse of the passion that seethed in their enigmatic, glittering depths. For the space of a heartbeat she was exposed to him, her naked emotions revealed to him with arousing potency. Brennermen was too dense to see it, and the children too young, but Luke couldn't miss it. There was a woman beneath her argumentative exterior, a soft, sensual woman. Instinctively, his nostrils flared, like a wolf scenting its prey.

A honking horn shattered their silent communion.

"School bus!" the children chorused.

"Lord, I haven't even got your lunches packed," Sarah said, turning to the counter and hastily stuffing sandwiches into the row of paper lunch bags.

Brennermen, seeing an opportunity for retreat, tried to slip out of the house. He got within a foot of the back door when he was unexpectedly collared from behind.

Brennermen was a big man, but Luke pulled him back as easily as a fisherman reels in a disappointing trout. "Listen up," he warned, his voice low and lethal. "If I hear of you saying anything—*anything*—unkind about Miss Gallagher or her children, I'll show you exactly how I got that three-state reputation for trouble. Understand?"

"Sure," Brennermen said, nodding emphatically. "You bet."

Luke gave the man a final bone-jarring shake, then opened the back door and unceremoniously shoved him out. Good riddance, he thought as he watched the man scurry away to his waiting Chevy. A man who picked on women and children deserved everything he got, Luke thought, but that wasn't the only reason he'd threatened Brennermen; it was, however, the only one he really understood. He was still confused, and intrigued, by the shock of awareness he'd shared with Sarah.

A friendly punch to his arm made him turn. Rafe stood beside him, a wide grin on his usually cynical face. "That was great, man."

"Sure was," a voice near his elbow agreed. Luke looked down and saw Micah at his side, his expression close to worship. "I've never seen Mr. Brennermen back down like that. You sure showed him."

"I . . . er," Luke started, unsure of what to say. He wasn't used to praise from kids or anyone else. "Anyone would have done it."

Jenny appeared beside Rafe. "No, they wouldn't," she said soberly. "You really helped us out. Thanks."

Luke looked at the children and saw the unfamiliar gratitude in their eyes. His intuition told him they weren't any more used to giving it than he was to taking it. He and these kids shared something. Maybe they weren't such a bad bunch. For kids.

The school bus sounded a second blast. The children grabbed their hastily packed lunches and headed out the door like a herd of buffalo. Yet despite their haste, they all spared at least a second to tell him they were glad he was staying. Even painfully shy Lyn mumbled a welcome, and Valerie, apparently forgiving him for last night's angry outburst, gave him a thousand-watt smile.

Minutes later they were gone. Luke was left alone in the kitchen with Sarah.

She stood at the sink, her back to him, rinsing off the children's breakfast dishes. Her graceful hands gave even that ordinary activity a new dignity. Luke took the moment to look her over and decided he liked what he saw. She'd traded her baggy pants and shirt for a faded cotton top and a pair of worn, well-fitting jeans. Neither left much of her figure to his imagination, and in Luke's seasoned opinion, that figure was a knockout. Her softly rounded hips swayed enticingly as she shifted her weight to place the dishes in the drainer. Luke doubted she'd appreciate hearing it, but that backside of hers was more suited to an exotic dancer than a mother of five.

The kid's praises had gone to his head like new wine. He walked up behind her, anticipating her gratitude. He smiled, cocksure. "It looks like I'm making a habit of rescuing you."

"I didn't ask for your help," Sarah said quietly, continuing to wash and rinse the dishes.

Luke stared at her, sobered by her cool response. Gratitude? He felt as if she'd just thrown dishwater in his face. "Hey, lady, I said I'd help you. You might at least say 'thank you.' "

She swung around. "Okay. Thank you. Thank you and good-bye." She met his gaze for a single, electrifying instant. Then she stepped away from the sink and reached for the dish towel hanging over the back of a kitchen chair. "I'll take you back to your truck now. With luck you can make Houston by late afternoon."

"Houston?"

"The oil-rig job, remember?" She stood with her back to him, ramrod-stiff. "You've got a wonderful job waiting for you there. I know you said you'd work for me to get Brennermen off my back. I appreciate the offer, but I can't take it."

Her response didn't make sense. Or maybe, he thought darkly, it made all the sense in the world. She'd wanted his help—practically begged for it— until Brennermen told her those rumors about him being a troublemaker.

His eyes narrowed ferally as he studied the taut-ness in her shoulders, her shifting, uneasy stance. She wasn't telling him the whole truth, but his hard-learned knowledge of human nature helped him fill in the blanks. She might not like Brennermen, but she trusted him. And because of the man's half-truths and innuendos, she didn't want Luke's kind of help anymore. His help, or anything else he had to offer.

Okay, maybe he wasn't a saint, but he'd made his offer in good faith. He deserved better than to be brushed off like some worthless drifter. Anger burned away his good intentions. For the first time in years he'd honestly tried to help someone, and she'd thrown his offer back in his face.

His jaw tightened into a hard, dangerous line. He didn't take that kind of treatment from others, and he damn well wasn't going to take it from her. He strode across the room until he stood directly behind her, so close that his breath stirred her hair. "Considering your alternatives," he said, his tone low and blatantly seductive, "I should think you'd *take* me any way you could get me."

He'd wanted to shock her, to force her to acknowl-edge him as a person, not some unimportant vagrant. He got that reaction. In spades.

She spun around, her eyes bright with angry chal-lenge. "Why you conceited, arrogant . . . oh—"

She placed her hands on his chest and shoved. Caught off-guard, Luke fell back against the edge of the kitchen counter, the hard surface biting into his still-aching bruise. Startled by the sudden pain, he sucked in his breath and swore.

"Oh, damn. I'm sorry," Sarah said, her anger dissipating at the sight of his suffering. "I forgot you were hurt. Let me take a look—"

"No," he ordered, backing away. He was in pain, but not that much pain, and being near her was already playing havoc with his better judgment. Lord knew what would happen if she touched him again with those incredibly sensual hands of hers. "I'll be fine. Just leave me alone."

She didn't seem convinced, but she obeyed him, dropping her arms to her side. Nervous concern clouded her eyes. "I'm really sorry. I didn't mean to hurt you. It seems all I ever do is cause you trouble."

Trouble? She didn't know the half of it. Those eyes of hers were working a strange sort of alchemy in his soul. The heart he'd thought immune to tender feelings hammered hard in his chest. Emotions that had lain dormant through years of neglect creaked steadily to life. He felt alive, really alive.

And it scared the hell out of him.

He settled back against the counter and sighed. "I guess I'm lucky you didn't have a sledgehammer."

"What?"

"Never mind." He raked his gaze over her, wondering how such a little package could pack such a wallop. "What were you before you bought this farm, anyway? A prizefighter?"

"A lawyer."

"Same thing," he commented, giving her the ghost of a grin.

She responded with a smile of her own, a soft, slightly uneven smile that made her look completely adorable. Luke felt as if someone had delivered a blow to his solar plexus. Smiles like that were more dangerous than dynamite. "Listen," he said carefully. "Those things Brennermen said about me. They're not true. At least, not entirely—"

"I know that," she interrupted. She brushed her unruly bangs off her face and continued, giving him her now-familiar, no-nonsense stare. "I've seen enough hardened criminals to recognize the type. You don't fit the profile. Believe me, cowboy, if I'd had even the slightest doubt about your character, you wouldn't have made it through my front door."

Her acceptance meant a great deal to Luke, more than he cared to admit. "Well, if you're so sure about me, why do you want me to go?"

"I don't—" She swallowed the rest of her sentence and dropped her gaze to the floor, apparently developing a sudden fascination for the silver tips of his boots. "I do not *want* you to go," she said carefully, "but I know it would be the best thing for you. You don't like kids. I've got five of them. You like freedom. This job will tie you to this farm for eight weeks. You'll hate it."

Luke said softly, "Why don't you let me be the judge of that?"

She glanced up quickly, her lips shaped in a sweet O of surprise. It struck him that she would never be pretty, that her chin was too strong and her mouth too generous. Yet she had a rarer kind of beauty, born of the strength and decency that welled up from deep inside her.

Once again he experienced that unsettling recognition, as if he were looking into a mirror. She'd been hurt deeply, perhaps as deeply as he had, but unlike him, she still had the ability to trust. That trust shimmered in her eyes like starlight, shining into his own jaded soul. If only he'd met someone like her years ago . . .

But he hadn't. He'd spent too many unrepentant years living hard and wild to change his ways now. And he damn sure didn't want to be anyone's hero.

He shifted uneasily and cleared his throat. "Brennermen's got you spooked," he said gruffly. "So what if you don't pass the inspection? They'll only slap you with a fine."

Although he wasn't looking at her, the strange affinity between them made him keenly aware of her every movement. He sensed rather than saw her grow very still. "You don't understand. I'm an adoptive parent, and a single one at that. The child-welfare board watches me like a hawk."

"So?" He shrugged, still not comprehending.

"So if I don't pass this inspection, Mr. Tyrell, there's a good chance I'll lose my children."

FOUR

"Tyrell?"

Sarah pushed the barn door open a bit wider and stepped through. Outside, the world shimmered with the heat and glory of a bright Texas afternoon, but in here the light was dim and sound muted. She blinked, adjusting her eyes to the relative darkness inside the structure. Faint sunlight filtered in through breaks in the barn's wooden siding, catching lazy swirls of chaff and dust in its rays. The air was hushed with an almost sacred silence. As a child, she'd sought out the shadowed peace of this place to escape her demanding parents and to think out her troubles. She wished her present problems were half as easy to solve.

"Tyrell?" she repeated hesitantly, hating to intrude upon the silence. "Are you in here?"

"In the loft!"

His voice rang through the stillness, disturbing the air, the dust, and her own uncertain heart. Sarah lifted her chin and watched his tall, lean form rise up from behind the hay bales and start toward the ladder. Bands of light cut across his body as he moved; they accented his power. Unbidden, she conjured up the image of a jungle cat, moving stealthily through the shadows toward its prey. It was a ridiculous notion, pure fantasy, but her breathing quickened all the same.

Luke grabbed the top rung of the ladder and swung down with an almost unholy ease. He dropped to the ground in front of her, the wooden floor creaking in protest from his unexpected weight. "What can I do for you?" he asked, his strong yet gentle voice caressing the silence.

Sarah bit back a totally inappropriate answer. "I finished fixing up the bunk room for you. It's right through there," she said, nodding to a small side door on her right. "It'll give you some privacy. You won't have to stay in the house with the kids . . . or with me."

"Thanks," he said simply, apparently not noticing the way her voice had faltered over the last two words.

His hooded eyes, unreadable in the dimness, flickered once over her figure. Sarah's chest constricted in a sudden, unfamiliar panic. She'd changed from her jeans to a pair of cutoffs, a concession to the afternoon warmth. But his gaze filled her with a very different kind of heat. Did he feel it too?

His actions gave her his answer. Apparently unimpressed, he bent down and casually wiped his palms on the rough denim of his work jeans.

Well, what did you expect? an inner voice asked. She'd known for a long time that her face and figure weren't exactly centerfold material. She weighed ten pounds more than all the fashion magazines said she should—fifteen pounds more than Mallory, her ex-husband's wife. Men, including Paul, always told her that they valued her for her mind rather than her body. Invariably, she'd politely thanked them for the compliment, resisting the urge to pull their tongues out by the roots. Why should she expect Luke's reaction to be any different?

Maybe because he *was* different.

His words brought her sharply back to reality. "I looked at the roof," he said, straightening. "It's in pretty good shape, considering its age. I think you can get by with just a patch job."

"Fine," Sarah said, glancing toward the rafters. It was better than staring at Luke. The dark blue T-shirt he'd changed into after they'd retrieved his truck was playing havoc with her senses. The thin material stretched tight across his chest, clearly defining the rock-hard muscles her fingers had skimmed over last night. Her hands burned with the memory of his skin, smooth and man-hot to her touch. Last night she'd been too worried about his injury to notice. Now she couldn't seem to notice anything else!

"Fine," she repeated, swallowing the unnatural dryness in her throat. "If we start on the roof tomorrow, we should be able to—"

"We? Roofing is a man's job."

Sarah's gaze leaped back to his face. "What?"

"You heard me," he said, crossing his arms over his chest. "I'll handle the roof. It's too dangerous for a woman—"

"And what am I supposed to do? Sit around and bake cookies?"

Luke's mouth twitched as if he were restraining a grin. "I don't know. Are your cookies any good?"

"That's not the point," Sarah answered, refusing to be distracted. "Two people can fix a roof twice as fast as one. We've got a deadline, and I intend to do anything and everything I can to meet it."

"Except roofing," Luke stated. Then, apparently unconcerned with her answer, he strode over to the far corner of the barn, where he focused his attention on the empty cattle stalls.

Sarah's temper flared. She'd met some narrow-minded men in her time, but Luke Tyrell beat them all. This was *her* farm, *her* home—and she wasn't about to let some arrogant, chauvinistic cowboy tell her how to run it. She stalked over to Luke, determined to tell him exactly what he could do with his sexist opinions. "Mr. Tyrell—"

"How many head of cattle have you got?"

The unexpected question took her by surprise. "Uh, two."

"Only two," Luke mused, rubbing his chin.

Sarah watched his movements, unaccountably fascinated by the way his fingers stroked his beard-roughened skin. The dark blond shadow reminded her all too clearly of the hair that dusted his chest. Light on his upper body, it grew darker as it approached his navel, and darker still as it neared his— Desperately, Sarah wrenched her gaze away from his hand. Dammit, she was supposed to be angry with him!

"Humm," Luke said, continuing to rub his chin. "Two hundred head. That's not much."

"No, not two hundred, only two," she corrected. "MacNeil and Lehrer are out in the side—"

"You've *named* them?"

"Well, of course. We couldn't just call them Steer One and Steer Two, could we?"

"How about Rib Steak and Rump Roast?"

Sarah gasped. "Don't you even suggest that. The kids love those animals. They're pets. We'll buy other steers to sell."

And she'd probably name the whole damn herd! Luke had never seen a place more in need of a foreman's firm hand. With no crops and no livestock to speak of, it was a wonder this place was still in business. If things didn't change soon, it was a sure bet she'd eventually lose her home to Brennermen. Not, he reminded himself, that it mattered to him. He'd agreed to help her, and he intended to keep his promise, but in two months he'd be moving on, Brennermen or no Brennermen. Corners would become just another one of the dozens of places he'd worked in the past ten years. And she'd become just another one of the owners he'd worked for.

"All right," he said gruffly, attributing his annoyance to her foolishness over the cattle. "If you want to treat cows as pets, that's your business. But keep your pets out of this barn for a while. Half of the slats in those stalls have rotted and need to be replaced. Can you handle a hammer?"

"I can handle anything you can," Sarah said, her eyes snapping with challenge. "Including *roofing*."

Luke gave a noncommittal 'humph,' wondering what he was going to do with her. The lady did not give up. He'd met some determined females in his time, but Sarah Gallagher took the prize. Still, he couldn't help admiring the way she always met her troubles head-on.

He also couldn't help admiring the way her sweet little backside filled out those cutoffs.

All at once he became aware of his surroundings. The barn was warm and quiet and filled with the heady scent of oiled leather along with new hay. A familiar tightness pulled at his abdomen. He and Sarah were alone, miles from anyone who might see or censure their actions. They could take a quick tumble in the hayloft without anyone being the wiser. He knew how to please a woman—she wouldn't regret the experience. And from the banked hellfire that burned in her eyes, he doubted he'd regret it either. . . .

Damn! He turned away abruptly. Was he crazy? Sarah Gallagher was many things, but a quick tumble wasn't one of them. She was the kind of woman a man came back to, not for just a night or a week, but for a lifetime. The kind of woman who had no place in his free-footed, solitary life.

He squatted down and made a show of examining the support poles for the hayloft. "You're damn lucky these aren't rotted too," he said tersely. "How'd you get stuck with this place, anyway?"

"I didn't get *stuck* with Corners. My great-aunt left the farm to me when she died. I spent my summers here as a child and always loved it. I know it needs a little work—"

"A little?" Luke scoffed. "Lady, that's like saying our country has a 'little deficit.' If you want my advice, you should take Brennermen's offer and move back to the city."

"That's exactly what my ex-husband told me," she said softly.

Luke rose to his full height, still trying to give the impression that he was checking out the loft support. But his mind was concerned with anything but. He recalled that Brennermen had mentioned Sarah was divorced, and the same thought struck him now as it had then. After gaining this caring woman's love, what man would be fool enough to give it up?

"Was that why you got divorced? Because your husband didn't want to live in the country?"

For a long moment she didn't answer. She stood still as stone in the center of the barn, hardly seeming to breathe. An errant sunbeam fell across her, wrapping her body in soft golden light. Normally a cynical man, Luke suddenly found himself thinking she seemed made of fire—a pure, cleansing blaze to burn away the deadwood in a man's soul. But the image of fire was illusory. When she spoke, her words sent a chill down his spine.

"My husband left me because he fell in love with another woman."

Luke was too stunned to say anything.

"It really wasn't his fault," Sarah continued with a lawyer's impartiality. "We'd grown apart. He had his life; I had mine. We didn't have anything in common anymore."

"So he went catting around because you didn't have anything in common," Luke said, his tone ripe with disgust.

"It wasn't like that," Sarah said sharply, finally showing some emotion.

Luke gave a short, derogatory snort. "Maybe they do things differently in the city," he drawled, as he leaned back against the support post and hooked his fingers through his belt loops. "But out here we don't much cotton to adultery. If my dad had ever played fast and loose with another woman, my mom would have gone after him with a shotgun. Not that she ever had to," he said, his mouth curving into an unfamiliarly tender smile. "Dad still worships the ground she walks on."

"You've got parents?"

"Of course I've got parents!" he said, straightening. "Two of the best. They live over in Galveston."

"I'm sorry," she said, apparently sensing she'd

offended him. "It's just that you seem like such a loner."

He was a loner. He liked it that way. But he also loved his parents, and talking about them reminded him he hadn't been over to see them in a long time. His mother never had learned how not to worry about him, he thought with a complex mixture of guilt and affection. Maybe after he finished this job, he'd take some time off and spend a couple of days—

"Your mother's name wouldn't happen to be 'Annie,' would it?"

The temperature in the barn dropped a measurable degree. "What makes you ask?"

He spoke slowly, with the lethal cadence of a gun being cocked. Too late, Sarah realized she'd made a mistake. "I . . . I heard you mention it in your sleep. I came into your room this morning to—"

"I don't give a damn *why* you came in."

In two steps he was beside her, staring her down with cold, deadly eyes. Shadows gathered around him, making him seem larger, even more threatening. She'd never been so aware of a man, his overwhelming strength, his sheer masculinity. His danger. Swallowing her sudden fright, she started to back away. He caught her upper arm, holding her fast.

His touch seared through her like a bolt of lightning.

"Never say that name again. Ever," he warned.

"But—"

"Ever!" he repeated, his voice a snarl. "And stay the hell out of my room when I'm sleeping. I don't like people spying on me."

"I wasn't spying!" Sarah answered, her anger rising to match his. Damn the man! She'd only been trying to help. But simple human kindness wasn't something a man like Luke Tyrell would understand. Not an overbearing, hard-edged, self-centered cretin like him. "Don't worry, Mr. Tyrell. From now on I intend to give you a wide berth, whether you're asleep or not!"

She twisted out of his grasp and stomped out of the barn. She needed fresh air and a chance to sort through the tumultuous feelings churning through her. Blinded by rage, she didn't see the overturned pail until it was too late. Her toe caught on its rim, and she pitched forward, crying out; her leg twisted under her as she landed on the ground.

She knew one moment of keening pain. Then Luke was beside her, turning her over with a gentleness that startled her even more than her fall. "Are you hurt?"

Hurt? She was in agony! His big, sure hands cradled her body against his chest, making her feel warm, safe, and, worst of all, cherished. Pressed against him, she had no choice but to feel his electric heat and to breathe in the rich salt-and-leather smell of his skin. It had been so long, so horribly long, since a man had held her like this. It took every ounce of her litigation-honed restraint not to bury her face in his shirt and drink in his raw, impossibly wonderful scent. "I'm f-fine," she said shakily.

"You don't sound fine," he stated curtly. Without warning, he scooped her up in his arms and carried her to the side door that led to the tack room. He leaned his shoulder against the recalcitrant door, the hinges protesting as it swung open under his greater strength.

Sarah had always considered the tack room to be a good-sized space, but it shrank visibly when Luke entered it. Tall and confident, he seemed to overwhelm everything he came in contact with. And everyone. Cradled in his powerful arms, Sarah felt her own strength ebbing away. She squeezed her eyes shut, wishing she could cut off the smell and feel of him as easily as she cut off her sight. She hated him for his lying hands, for the counterfeit tenderness that couldn't be genuine after his recent anger. She hated him for splintering her common sense as easily as a woodsman splits logs.

He set her down on the narrow bed. Her eyes still shut, Sarah gripped the covers, praying he'd go away and leave her and her traitorous body in peace. He didn't. A scant second later she felt the bed shift under his weight as he sat down on the far end. Strong fingers circled her ankle.

Her eyes flew open. "What are you doing?"

"Lie still, Sarah," he commanded.

Sarah. He'd never called her by her first name before, and the unconscious intimacy unnerved her.

She'd heard her name spoken hundreds of times, but it sounded different when Luke said it. Soft and special . . . and somehow right.

He slipped off her sneaker, ignoring her protest. Then, frowning with concentration, he gingerly rotated her ankle. "How does this feel?"

She didn't dare tell him. Fire raced through her veins, melting her from the inside out. His fingers brushed her unprotected sole with exquisite tenderness. Sweet pleasure surged through her. She bit back a moan, promising herself that she'd never take her feet for granted again. At least she wouldn't, provided she survived Luke's examination. "It feels . . . fine."

Without looking up, Luke shook his head. "For a lawyer you've got a pretty limited vocabulary. What about this?"

His hand advanced to her calf, expertly testing her muscles. Sarah had thought that nothing could be more erotic than the feel of his knowing hands on her vulnerable foot. She'd been wrong. Pressed into the naked skin of her leg, his warm, steel-strong fingers caressed her with the intimacy of a kiss. Hot and cold geysers erupted through her, and her heart beat like thunder. She bit her bottom lip, focusing on the small pain to steady her control. But as his hands steadily approached the sensitive flesh at the back of her knee, she knew the pain wouldn't stop her from making a complete fool of herself.

Marshaling the last of her strength, she pulled her leg out of his grasp and skittered like a crab to the far side of the bed. "Stop it," she said, hardly finding enough air in her lungs to rasp out the words. "Stop touching me like that."

For a moment he looked shocked. Then a bleak, all-too-familiar coldness frosted over his ice-blue eyes. "Lady," he said through gritted teeth, "believe me, there're plenty of things I'd rather do with my time than feel up your calf."

Of course there are, she thought, conscious of the hot blush of embarrassment creeping up her cheeks. She knew all too well that her body didn't have the necessary equipment to stir a man. Paul's defection to pretty, vacuous Mallory had more than proved that point. The passion Luke's touch had ignited was completely one-sided. She'd made a fool of herself after all.

"I'm sorry," she said, ignoring her pride for her lawyer's sense of justice. "I was wrong. You were only trying to be kind."

His hooded eyes narrowed dangerously. He looked at her, through her, cutting out her secrets with his steel-edged gaze. His eyes seemed to strip off her clothes and the skin underneath. She felt naked, exposed, and incredibly, horribly aroused. Instinct told her to get off that bed and find a deep dark hole to hide in. But that was the coward's choice. Instead, she lifted her chin and met his eyes with all the courage she could muster.

Then, absurdly, his mouth pulled up in the barest

hint of a smile. "Well, maybe I wasn't trying to be all that kind," he said.

His final word was swallowed up by the ringing phone. Grateful for the interruption, Sarah rose from the bed and walked over to the extension her aunt had installed in the room during the sixties. There is a God, she thought as she picked up the ancient receiver.

A minute of conversation made her revise that opinion. She hung up the receiver, stunned by the words she'd never thought to hear again.

She was so distressed, she didn't realize Luke was beside her until she felt his firm, calming hand on her shoulder. "What's wrong?"

She knew she should be cautious, that she shouldn't put her trust in a man who had wandering feet and a reputation for trouble. But she didn't care. He was here, and he was strong. For the moment that was enough. She turned around and looked up at him, not bothering to brush away the tears in her eyes. "That was Lyn calling from school. Jenny's been taken to the principal's office." She paused, swallowing the knot of fear in her throat before adding, "She's been accused of stealing by Cathy Brennermen."

FIVE

"You're sure you've told me absolutely everything?" Sarah asked.

"Everything," Jenny promised shakily. She sat board-stiff in the wooden chair facing the principal's desk, her expression proud and defiant. Only her wavering voice betrayed her fear. "I didn't take nothing."

Sarah heard a snicker from the far side of the room. Glancing up, she saw the sneer on Cathy Brennermen's pretty, pouty face. Sarah had dealt with all kinds of kids during her tenure as public defender, but she'd never met a child she completely loathed. Until now.

A deeper, entirely different kind of voice came from the other side of the room. "Mrs. Kochakian," Luke said in his deceptively lazy drawl, "in a school this big, there's bound to be more than one kid with sticky fingers. Maybe someone else took the watch."

Warmth spread through Sarah. Luke had insisted

on following her to the school, volunteering to take the rest of her children back home in his truck in case she had to stay with Jenny. "Staying" meant a trip to the local police station if they couldn't clear Jenny of these charges, but Luke didn't go into that. He simply pulled his truck up behind hers and yelled for her to go slow because he couldn't afford a speeding ticket on what she was paying him. His stupid joke had given her the only smile she'd had since Lyn's distressing phone call.

Now he stood near the office's single window, one hip propped on the sill, his ancient Stetson pulled down to shield his eyes from the glare of the setting sun. In his scuffed boots and tattered denim jacket he looked to Sarah like a slightly tarnished white knight—and so damn handsome, it took her breath away. She was still incredibly confused about her feelings for him, but she couldn't afford to let them distract her now. Jenny needed her full attention, and every ounce of her lawyer's wit.

Mrs. Kochakian's next words brought home the point with a vengeance. "Of course, it's possible that someone else took Cathy's watch, Mr. Tyrell," she said. "But Jenny was the only one near the hall lockers at the time. And she does have a history of petty theft."

"That was years ago!" Sarah cried. "She hasn't taken a thing since she's come to live with me."

"Still, we must take precautions," the principal replied. At least, that's what she said aloud. Her tightly laced fingers and pursed mouth implied a different answer. *Once a thief, always a thief.*

Icy fingers of dread tightened around Sarah's heart. She'd seen innocent kids convicted before and knew what happened to them once they got a record. All too often it started them on a downward spiral that continued into adulthood. True, a juvenile offender's official files were closed once the child reached adulthood, but the unofficial scars could last a lifetime.

Sarah's mind flashed back to the broken girl she'd met almost two years ago—an angry, hopeless eleven-year-old who was determined to hate the world before it had a chance to hate her. Through patience and love Sarah had begun to rebuild Jenny's belief in herself, but that belief was still as delicate as gossamer. A conviction now, especially for something she didn't do, could rip the fragile web to shreds.

Sarah couldn't let that happen. She couldn't!

"Please," she said, bracing her palms on the principal's desk and leaning forward. "Please, I swear to you Jenny didn't do this. Just let us go home. I'm sure the watch will turn up."

Luke cleared his throat. "Sarah, I think Mrs. Kochakian might need more—"

"You stay out of this," Sarah warned, flashing him a dagger-filled glance. "She's not your child!"

Luke stiffened. Instinctively, he knew that it wasn't Sarah who lashed out at him, but the lioness protecting her threatened cub. The knowledge didn't stop her claws from hurting. "Fine," he said tightly as he pushed off the sill. "I'll wait for you outside."

He left the office and strode down the corridor, letting his long legs choose his course down the wide hallways. His quick, heavy steps rang like gunshots in the silence. The sounds matched his mood. Cold. Harsh. Unforgiving.

Damn her! Twice this afternoon he'd offered to help her, first when he'd tended her leg in the barn, and now, when he'd tried to smooth things over for Jenny. He'd planned to defuse the steadily increasing tension in the room by flattering the principal a bit, maybe enough to buy them some time to look for Cathy's missing watch. But Sarah hadn't believed he'd take Jenny's side, any more than she'd believed in his genuine concern for her possible injury. She didn't trust him to help her, despite the way he's stood by her and her kids against Brennermen this morning. Hell, she didn't trust him, period.

"I don't need this," he grumbled, slowing his steps. He had a good job waiting for him in Houston. And he was sure that if he looked in the right places, he could find a not-so-good woman waiting for him there as well. A woman who wouldn't throw his offers of help back in his face, who wouldn't ask questions, who wouldn't care or make him care.

A woman who wouldn't ask him about Annie.

He came to a stop at the end of the corridor. Hallways stretched out on either side of him, mirroring the decision he had to make in his own life. Right or left, stay or go? Which way should he turn?

All at once he heard voices coming from some-where along the right-hand corridor. Kids' voices.

"You're doing it wrong," a young, anxious voice protested.

"I am not," a slightly deeper voice replied. "I've watched guys do this lots of times."

"But it's not working. Maybe if you hold it like a scalpel . . ."

Scalpel? Most kids might know what a scalpel was, but few of them would know how to hold it, and Luke could think of only one who might: Micah. Frowning, he turned right and headed down the hallway, using a hunter's stealthy gait. Two boys stood in front of a locker.

"I think I've got it," Rafe said, turning the pick in the lock.

Micah pushed his glasses up on his nose and leaned closer. "Don't scratch the lock. You'll leave evidence."

"I *know* that," Rafe answered. He twisted the pick around a few times, then stepped back. "Okay, that's it," he said and reached for the locker's handle. The door didn't budge.

"Not again." Micah moaned. "We'll never get this thing open."

"Don't say that," Rafe said angrily. "We've got to get this open for Spot's sake. If we don't, they'll—"

He stopped abruptly as Luke's long shadow fell over them. Two pairs of eyes shot up and met the tall cowboy's steady, unamused gaze. "And just what do you boys think you're doing?"

Rafe and Micah shuffled nervously. "Nothing," they said in unison.

Luke tipped back his hat. "It doesn't look like nothing. If you kids are doing what I think you are, you're buying into a world of hurt—"

"We don't care!" Rafe stated. "We're not gonna let Cathy frame Spots."

Frame? Luke thought. That was an angle he hadn't figured on. One look at Brennermen's daughter had told him she was as smug and self-centered as her father. The apple hadn't fallen far from the tree. But to maliciously accuse a classmate . . . "What makes you think she's framing your sister?"

"Because she hates us," Rafe said. "Her dad's been trying to get rid of us since we moved here."

"And she's still mad about Curt," Micah added.

Luke's gaze swung back and forth between the boys, trying to follow their conversation. "Who's Curt?"

"Cathy's older brother," Rafe explained. "He went to Annapolis last fall, but during senior year he wanted to go out with Lyn big time. She wouldn't give him the time of day."

"Because he's a jerk," Micah added.

"Yeah," Rafe agreed. "Captain of the football team. He thought he was so cool."

"Until Lyn told him to get lost."

"Boy, was he p . . . angry," Rafe said. "And Cathy took it as a big insult to her family."

Micah nodded. "She's been out to get us ever since. Only she's never made it stick before. Until now. That's why we're breaking into Jenny's locker."

Luke looked at the boys in surprise. "Jenny's locker? I thought this was Cathy's."

Rafe shook his head. "The principal already searched Cathy's locker and found zip. But Cathy's hinted a couple of times that they should check out Spot's locker. We're pretty sure she slipped her watch inside when Jenny wasn't looking. It's the sort of rotten thing she'd do."

Remembering Cathy's sly expression in the principal's office, Luke had to agree. He pondered the deluge of words the boys had just delivered. They were too scared to be telling him anything but the truth—scared, he realized, for Jenny. He felt something close to envy. What he wouldn't give to be that innocent again, and to care about someone as much as the boys obviously cared about their sister. To love someone again . . .

His mind clamped down ruthlessly on the thought.

"Look, boys," he said sternly, "the last thing your sister needs is for you to end up in the principal's office alongside her. You'd better get out of here before someone catches you."

"You're not gonna turn us in?" Micah said, his mouth open in surprise.

Somehow it hurt Luke that Micah believed he would do such a thing. Almost unconsciously, he reached out and gave the boy's chin a playful punch, mirroring a gesture his father had used on him when he was a boy. "Your only crime is loving your sister. No one's going to put you behind bars for that."

"What about Jenny?" Rafe asked bitterly. "Are they going to put her behind bars?"

Luke glanced down at the older boy and saw a man's worth of experience behind his hard, gunmetal-gray eyes. "Not if I can help it," he promised brusquely. He nodded in the general direction of the office and the visitors' lounge where Lyn and Valerie waited. "Now get out of here before I change my mind and turn you in after all."

After the sound of the boys' footsteps had faded into silence, Luke turned back to the locker. He noted the manufacturer's name, recognizing it as an industrial brand widely used throughout the South on ranches and oil rigs. He placed his hand on the hinge seam, carefully running his fingers along the edge until he found a shallow, almost invisible indentation. Then he drew back his arm and gave the spot a sharp, resounding hit with the heel of his hand.

The locker popped open. And there, sitting on top of a biology book, was Cathy's "stolen" watch.

Why that vicious, vindictive little cat, Luke thought as he pocketed the watch. He closed the locker with a bang, then set off down the hallway at a pace just short of running. It took him only a few short minutes to reach the office. Through the glass-partition wall he saw that Sam Brennermen had arrived and was engaged in a heated discussion with Sarah. Even at a distance Luke could see her proud shoulders begin to droop under Brennermen's onslaught. A hard, fierce anger filled his gut. He grabbed the knob and gave the door a mighty shove.

"You again," Brennermen said, clearly not at all pleased to see Luke.

Well, the feeling's mutual, Luke thought. Smiling slowly, he reached into his jacket pocket and pulled out the watch, taking extreme pleasure as he dangled it in front of Brennermen's beet-red face. "Is this what you're looking for?"

Brennermen sputtered like the loose lid on a boiling kettle. "Wh-where did you find it?"

"In the hallway," Luke answered. Then, casting a meaningful glance at Cathy, he added, "on the floor."

Cathy's mouth dropped open in surprise. She started to speak, but no sound came out. Luke had figured as much, since she could hardly accuse him of breaking into Jenny's locker without incriminating herself. Her eyes narrowed to weasellike slits, giving him a glimpse of the mean-spirited brat lurking behind the angelic exterior. He had no trouble believing she'd frame Jenny for pure spite. The kid was poison.

Luke's thoughts ended abruptly as he felt something soft and warm settle against his stomach. He looked down, and saw Jenny hugging his waist, her face pressed into his stomach. Startled, he tried to back away. She only hugged tighter.

"Thank you," she said, her words muffled against his middle.

Oh hell, he thought, feeling completely perplexed by the situation. A handshake he could deal with, but a hug! Children did not throw their arms around notorious Luke Tyrell. He was a hard man. A cold man. And at the moment a very confused man.

Desperate, he cast his gaze around the room and met Sarah's eyes. Amusement gleamed in their depths, informing him that she understood his predicament but had no intention of lifting a finger to help him. Angry words formed in his mind, but he couldn't get them past his lips. Astonished, he realized why.

He was grinning too hard to let them.

Things quickly returned to normal at the Gallagher household—or as normal as they ever got. By early evening Jenny had regained most of her confidence, and by the end of dinner she was back to bickering with Rafe as if nothing had happened. Everyone behaved as they usually did, including, unfortunately, Luke.

The smile they'd shared in the principal's office was nestled in a secret place in Sarah's heart. Luke's wide, boyish grin had revealed the warm, compassionate soul hidden beneath his hardened, cynical exterior. For an unforgettable moment Sarah had felt that they were the only two people in the world. Then Luke's smile had died, and his forbidding exterior returned, shutting her out like a homeless person on a cold winter's night.

She'd spoken to him several times that evening, trying to thank him for finding Cathy's watch. She'd received only curt, one-syllable answers for her trouble. By the time they'd finished dinner, her sense of loss had been replaced by complete annoyance. The man was impossible! But, impossible or not, he had helped clear Jenny, and, by God, Sarah was going to thank him for it. Whether he wanted to hear it or not!

Luke left for his room directly after dinner. It took Sarah almost an hour to clean the kitchen and get the kids committed to finishing their homework, but after she was done, she started out after Luke. She left the kitchen and stepped out onto the darkened porch, intending to head straight for the barn and thank Luke in the same one-syllable words he'd been handing to her all evening.

The tack-room window was pitch-black.

Perhaps he had gone to bed. She wrapped her fingers around a column on the porch. She should have been pleased at the thought of not having to see him again that night. Instead, she felt as if she'd been robbed of something precious and irreplaceable. *Sarah, be careful.* . . .

Sighing, she leaned her forehead against the column and gave herself up to the moment. She took in a deep breath of the night air, rich with the damp, dark smells of spring. Sarah closed her eyes, imagining that her great-aunt was standing beside her, doling out advice in large, generous spoonfuls. She could use some of the old woman's wisdom now. *Aunt Connie, what am I going to do about my feelings for—*

"Nice night," commented a laconic voice beside her.

Sarah's head jerked up. Turning, she saw Luke sitting not ten feet away from her on the old porch swing. It was hardly surprising she'd missed him. She swallowed, fighting down a strange, oddly pleasant sort of panic. "I . . . didn't know you were out here."

"You sorry I am?"

"No," she said quickly, wondering why she suddenly felt so awkward. "In fact, I came out here looking for you."

The swing squeaked faintly in the darkness. "That so?"

Damn the man! Did he always have to sound so infuriatingly composed when simply being near him made her feel as if she were standing on the edge of a high cliff? *Handle it, counselor*, she warned herself. She cleared her throat. "I never got a chance to thank you for helping clear Jenny."

"I didn't do much."

"Nonsense," she said, piqued that he would belittle his important role in saving her daughter. "If you hadn't found Cathy's watch, the police would have—"

"I don't want to talk about it," he stated gruffly. "I'd appreciate it if you didn't mention it again."

What was the matter with the man? Most people enjoyed hearing their actions praised, whether they deserved it or not. Luke deserved praise more than most, yet he disregarded it. Confused, she peered into the shadows that surrounded him. "Why don't you want to talk about it?"

"Because—" he began angrily, then stopped. The porch swing shrieked in protest as he came to his feet. He walked over to the edge of the porch and leaned heavily on the railing, then raised his eyes to stare into the dark heart of the night. "I didn't find the watch. I broke into Jenny's locker, where Cathy had planted it, and stole it back." He breathed a long sigh of frustration before adding, "I guess you'd call that 'tampering with the evidence.' Brennermen was right when he told you I was trouble."

Sarah said nothing.

Hell, Luke, what did you expect? She was a lawyer, as honest as they came. She wouldn't tolerate dishonesty from anyone—certainly not from a man who had a long-standing reputation as a lawbreaker. Steeling himself, he glanced over at her, expecting to see her disgust for him mirrored on her face.

Instead, she was smiling. "Damn, I wish I'd thought of breaking in like that."

Luke stared at her, deciding this time she'd truly lost her mind. "But I broke the law."

"Cowboy, I'd have robbed Fort Knox if it would have helped Jenny." She unwrapped her fingers from around the pole and walked over to him. Laying her small, fine-boned hand on top of his larger, coarser one, she said softly, "Thank you for saving my daughter."

Her touch was light and companionable, but its effect on Luke was anything but. Passion ripped through him. Every nerve in his body sizzled to life, filling him with a desire so sudden and intense, it almost choked him. Stunned, he realized he wanted her, wanted her more than he'd ever wanted a woman in his life. Memories lashed him—the touch of her gentle, incredibly erotic fingers stroking his side the previous night, the feel of her silk-smooth, firmly muscled leg against the palm of his hand this afternoon. There was nothing nice, caring, or even decent about the things he wanted to do to her, with her, *in her*. . . .

Lust flayed him. He closed his eyes, fighting against the pain and glory of it, moaning softly from the struggle. Instantly, her hand tightened on his, torturing him even more.

"Are you all right?" she asked, her voice full of innocent concern. "Is it your side again?"

It was definitely not his *side* causing the problem, and if he didn't get out of here quick, he doubted even the dark could hide what was. Gathering the last of his scattered wits, he pulled his hand roughly out from under hers and stalked off across the porch toward the steps. "Need some sleep," he mumbled as his feet hit the ground. He couldn't trust himself to say more.

"Of course," she agreed. "It's been a full day. But before you go, tell me what you want for breakfast tomorrow."

Luke stopped. Breakfast? Hell, if he had any brains, he wouldn't be around here come breakfast. He'd be hightailing it back to his safe, solitary life, where the only things he desired were enough money to fill his tank with gas and his belly with food. If he had any brains at all . . .

"Luke?" she called from the porch behind him. "Are you sure you're all right?"

He didn't turn back. He didn't have to. He knew how she'd look, poised at the top of the steps, her face washed by the pale light of the quarter-moon. He knew her brow would be furrowed in concern for him, a simple, honest concern that no one had wasted on him in years. And he knew, with a granite certainty, that he'd kill anyone who tried to hurt this brave, good woman. Including himself.

He looked up, silently asking God why He'd let him step into this honey-sweet bear trap of a household. But the Almighty was singularly quiet, and the twinkling stars seemed to laugh at his folly. Grimly, Luke realized he was on his own with this one. Again.

Well, as long as he was stuck here, he might as well make the best of it. "Eggs," he said boldly, as if challenging the heavens to deny him. "Three of them. With a tall stack of pancakes on the side."

SIX

"A month left," Sarah murmured as she studied the kitchen calendar. Only a month left until the building inspector visited her farm. Which also meant, of course, that *he'd* been living at Corners for a month now.

Sarah busied herself with the last of the breakfast dishes and tried to concentrate on something besides her hired hand. But the more she tried to fight it, the more Luke's image forced itself into her mind. It didn't make sense. He was obnoxious. He was annoying. He was— She sighed, wiping her warm, sudsy forearm across her brow as she admitted the truth to herself. *He was wonderful.*

He knew more about farming than all her agricultural pamphlets and textbooks put together. He used the technical names for plants and equipment, making her wonder if he'd studied agricultural engineering in the past, but when she asked him about it, he closed up tighter than an unshelled walnut. Still, he shared his knowledge willingly and helped her to map out a planting schedule that would put Corners in the black in less than two years. Last week he'd rented the equipment and laid the seed for her first cash crop, though he'd absolutely refused to let her drive the tractor. Apparently, planting, like roofing, was "a man's job." She'd informed the social worker in Dallas, Amanda Graves, about Luke's being hired, but hadn't heard a word from the older woman about her report.

She and Luke still argued on a regular basis. She was an independent career woman and he was a die-hard chauvinist. Clashes were inevitable. Yet she had to admit that sometimes she liked the way he refused to let her do the more demanding repairs, treating her like a fragile lady of the last century rather than a co-worker. It was ridiculous, of course. Sarah's nickname among the other attorneys around the courthouse had been the Iron Maiden. She had never been anyone's hothouse flower. Certainly, her ex-husband had never thought of her that way. But whenever she was around Luke, she went all soft and mushy inside, like one of those hard candies with the chewy centers. In his brash, pigheaded, and brusquely endearing way, Luke made her feel special. No, more than special . . .

Annie, I love you.

The memory of Luke's dream-fevered words shocked her back to reality. *Talk about stupid!* She pulled off her apron and started for the kitchen door. Luke was in love with Annie, and his refusal even to speak her name told Sarah how deep his love ran. And, if she doubted it, she had only to remember the way he'd snapped at her when she'd dared to mention his precious Annie's name. She'd already made the mistake of loving a man who loved someone else; she suffered still the pain and humiliation of her ex-husband's betrayal. She'd have to be the world's biggest fool to buy into that kind of hell again.

A tuneless whistle caught her attention. She glanced out the open kitchen window and saw Luke bent over the porch steps, replacing the rotted boards. Schwarzenegger, the only one of her stray mongrels who even approximated a watchdog, sat nearby, his tail occasionally making a contented swipe as he watched Luke intently.

Against her will, Sarah found herself studying the long, lean cowboy with a fascination rivaling Schwarzy's. Luke swung his heavy hammer with fluid grace, defining every rock-solid muscle in his well-tanned arms. He wore a white sleeveless shirt that stretched across his chest like a second skin, revealing a great deal more than it concealed. Sarah closed her eyes, fighting a sudden bout of vertigo. How could she let him get to her like this? She sprinted upstairs to her bathroom to bathe her face in cold water. She had to calm down and cool off before she faced him.

The task proved easier said than done. While running the cold water, she discovered the drain was clogged. Great, she thought as she spun the faucet to the closed position, the beginning of another perfect day. She considered calling Luke, but the idea of facing him at this particular moment turned her knees to the consistency of Jell-O. Besides, during the past month she'd assisted him with dozens of repairs and learned a great deal in the process. Surely, she was capable of fixing a sink.

Her confidence died quickly. The old pipes were rusted in place, and no amount of force or banging would move them. Clenching her teeth, she gathered her strength and gave the pipe one last, shoulder-straining try. It didn't budge a millimeter. Frustrated, she threw down the wrench and uttered the foulest curse she could think of.

"Taking lessons from Jenny?"

Sarah froze as two long, denim-clad legs stepped into view. "I thought you were fixing the steps," she said in a small voice.

"I was until I heard you banging away up here," he answered. He hunkered down beside her, peering into the darkness beneath the sink. "What's the problem?"

The problem is that your leg is pressed against my thigh, she thought, fighting the sweet burning that spilled through her at Luke's touch. Forcing herself to move slowly, she inched out from under the sink and sat beside him, drawing her legs away from his in the process. "The sink's clogged," she explained, pleased at how calm she sounded. "I'm trying to get the curvy thing off to see what's blocking it."

Luke gave her a pained expression. "That 'curvy thing' is called a 'trap'. And if you don't treat it real gentle, you could pull the whole sink down around your ears."

"Oh," she said, guiltily thinking what a disaster it would have been if she'd inadvertently ripped out the sink. They had enough repairs to complete before the inspection as it was.

Luke held out his hand. "Give me the wrench. I'll take a look at it."

Centuries of masculine tolerance for feminine ineptness were packed into his tone. All at once Sarah felt the devil rise up in her. "Oh, would you?" she said breathlessly, batting her lashes frantically as she handed him the wrench. "I do so love watching big, strong men wrestle with nasty plumbing."

Luke grinned at her outrageous sarcasm. Sarah had determined that he smiled about as often as the sun went through an eclipse. The effect was just as spectacular.

While Luke worked on the pipes, she wandered into her bedroom, trying to turn her mind to other things. But her gaze kept straying back to his lower body, studying it with a bold hunger that both embarrassed and thrilled her. The man should be arrested for what he did to a pair of jeans. They were tighter than they'd been when he arrived at Corners, and it filled her with honest pleasure to know that her good cooking had added needed pounds to his too-lean frame. She wondered with unaccustomed cattiness if he'd enjoyed Annie's cooking as much as hers.

Good Lord, I'm becoming as bad as Cathy Brennermen.

"Got it!" Luke yelled suddenly. He scooted out from under the sink, triumphantly holding a small blob of gray gunk.

Sarah stopped at the door and made an unpleasant face. "What is it?" she asked hesitantly.

Luke pulled a bandanna out of his back pocket and wiped the bulk of the slime from the tiny object. "It looks like . . . a dinosaur?"

"Benny!" she cried, immediately forgetting her revulsion and reaching for the plastic toy. "Benny the brontosaurus. Valerie's been looking for him for a week."

Luke looked from the toy to her and back to the toy. Sarah steeled herself for the expected insult. Here it comes, she told herself. Here comes the cynical remark where he makes fun of me for letting Valerie stuff toys down the sink.

But the remark never came. Instead, Luke's expression became serious, and he wiped the toy clean with astonishing care. "Better run it through the dishwasher," he said as he dropped it in her outstretched palm. "We wouldn't want Valerie catching anything from this gunk."

And then he smiled again.

Oh dear Lord. She felt a tiny earthquake shudder through her. It was one thing to keep her distance from the hard-bitten loner, from someone who thought only of himself and didn't give a damn about anyone else. But how could she resist a man who put up with her children's failings, who smiled instead of scowled, and who was working his way into all their hearts? She wanted to reach out and cup his beard-roughened cheek, to stroke her sensitive thumb across his lips and gentle his strength with her softness. She felt a crazy yearning for things she couldn't name—things she didn't dare name—but that she wanted so much, it made her ache inside.

Things she would never receive from a man who loved someone else.

Reality clamped down on her heart like a cold steel vise. When was she going to learn? "I'll take this to the dishwasher," she said dully.

Luke watched her swiftly retreating figure, his smile dissolving into a harsher, grimmer expression. *Damn, lady, you think you could be a little less obvious about wanting to get the hell away from me?*

Luke rose to his feet and shoved his strong fingers through his hair in frustration, a frustration that had been building inside him for almost a month. He could understand Sarah's initial wariness—his reputation didn't inspire trust. But after four solid weeks of working together she could at least try to cut him some slack.

He'd worked like a dog from sunup to sundown without a word of complaint. He'd given the local nightspots a wide berth, avoiding all possibilities of the trouble Brennermen had claimed he was famous for.

He'd even been civil to her children, though he had to admit he was beginning to like the little hell-raisers, especially since the younger kids had started to follow him around like puppies.

Yet, despite all his efforts, she still avoided him as if he carried the plague.

He looked around at the bathroom, at the dainty white finger towels with roses along the bottom, and at the lace curtains that looked as if they'd fall apart if he so much as breathed on them. They were the most ridiculously useless things he'd ever seen, yet their impracticality coaxed his solemn lips into a smile. It was comforting in some inexplicable way to know that his wary, no-nonsense employer had a frivolous side.

His face broke into an outright grin when he spotted the line of bottles and jars on the shelf right beneath the bathroom mirror. Feeling like a kid in a candy shop, he reached for the brightest jar, screwed off the top, and took a sniff. The damn stuff smelled like fruit salad.

"Women," he murmured, his tone hovering between reverence and annoyance. He read the label, wondering what in the heck "emulsifying" meant and where on the body it took place. Intriguing images came to mind. His grin broadened wickedly as he imagined other intriguing activities he'd like to indulge in with her.

"What are you doing?"

Luke looked up to see Sarah staring at him from the bathroom doorway. He sagely decided to keep his thoughts on "emulsification" to himself, and said good-naturedly, "I was trying to figure out whether you eat this stuff or wear it."

She didn't appear to appreciate his humor. In fact, she looked as white as one of her bathroom towels. "Please," she said quietly. "Put it back."

Luke heard the unmistakable burr of pain in her voice. Somehow his innocent teasing had touched a nerve. He closed the jar and set it back on the shelf. "Sarah," he said in the tone he used to gentle calves and colts, "what's the matter?"

For a moment she continued staring, embarrassment burning in her eyes. Then she sighed and crossed her arms in front of her, a defensive gesture she hadn't used with him since the day he'd saved Jenny.

"I . . . I suppose you think it's silly. Paul certainly did. He'd ask me why I needed so many beauty aids when . . ." She swallowed, then shrugged her shoulders in a way that tried for indifference and failed. "Well, I'm not exactly model material, am I?"

Luke had a gift for divining the truth behind people's words. The talent had saved his skin more than once over the past ten years. Listening to Sarah, he saw a bleak picture of a soft woman married to an insensitive man, the kind of bastard who'd use every opportunity to destroy her confidence, even a pot of face cream. Luke wished he had five minutes alone with Sarah's ex-husband. He'd teach him a thing or two about destruction.

It was easy, so very easy, to destroy the fragile things of this world. A deep ache twisted within him, reminding him of one vulnerable soul who would never be saved. But Sarah could be. Slowly, he reached out his hand to her. "Sarah, come here."

She lifted her chin defiantly, obviously still wary. "Why?"

Luke wasn't in the mood to play twenty questions. His gaze locked on hers with a tangible force. "Come here," he commanded.

This time she obeyed.

He took her by the shoulders. He could feel the tension in her and knew that inside she was wound tighter than a watch spring. He prayed it was because of his teasing and not a reaction to his touch. Gently, he turned her around to face the bathroom mirror. "I'm not much for speeches," he said, choosing his words with uncommon care, "but I know a pretty woman when I see one."

"That's kind of you to say, but—"

"I'm not being *kind*," he barked, frustrated by her reluctance to see what was obvious to anyone with eyes in his head. "You've got soft hair, pretty eyes, and a sex—that is, you've got a real nice figure."

"Really?" she asked, clearly intrigued by his viewpoint. "Men usually tell me I've got a wonderful personality and leave it at that."

The corner of Luke's stern mouth twitched. "I don't know why they would. You've got a lousy personality."

She flashed him a smile bright enough to outshine the July sun. Its heat settled inside him, thawing places where he'd never hoped to feel warmth again. Unfortunately, it wasn't the only heat stirring within him. Too late he realized how close they were, how only a few scant inches separated him from her enticing backside. It was impossible not to notice how well they fit together.

"I'm sorry I snapped at you," Sarah said, her matter-of-fact tone telling him she hadn't the faintest notion of what he was thinking. "It was rude of me, especially after you helped me out with the sink. You've been very kind."

Kind. He was starting to hate that word. "Kind" was something you called doting uncles and pet dogs—not notorious Luke Tyrell. Well, he wasn't her uncle, and he sure as hell wasn't anyone's pet. He was a man, with a man's hunger for the woman who stood near him. Ancient appetites rose up in him. He sniffed the air, inhaling the softly intoxicating fragrances of her hair and skin, and the darker, richer smell that belonged to Sarah alone. She got to him faster than any woman he'd ever known. He closed his eyes, hoping to kill the intensity of his arousal. It only made it stronger.

"Do you know that you smell like a forest after a rainstorm?" he whispered, unable to keep the words inside him any longer. "All fresh and clean, but also tangled and a little wild."

"Is that good?" she whispered back.

Eyes still closed, he heard the slight tremor in her

voice. He was getting to her too. He opened his eyes and saw a haze of desire clouding her bewitching green gaze. She was caught fast in the same honey-eyed spell that he was. His conscience told him no gentleman would take advantage of a vulnerable woman.

He reminded his conscience, he was no gentleman.

"*Very* good," he assured her. He reached up and stroked the dark silk of her hair, loving the sound of the small catch in her breathing. She was so sweet, so artlessly arousing. Recalling how her ex-husband had trampled on her sweetness made him madder than anything had in a long time.

Under his hand he felt her stiffen.

"Is something wrong?" she asked. "You look angry."

"I am, but not with you. I was thinking about that mule-stupid guy you married. He must have been deaf, dumb, and blind to let you go."

She smiled again, but it was a forced effort, lacking its former radiance. "That's kind of you to say, but—"

She gasped in shock as Luke grabbed her shoulders. "Listen up, lady, and listen good," he said. "I am not being kind. I have never been 'kind' where beautiful women are concerned, and I'm damn sure not about to start now."

"Beautiful?" she asked in a hushed tone. "You think I'm beautiful?"

Luke made a sound of exasperation. "What in blazes do they teach you in the city? Yes, I think you're beautiful, and not just because of the way you look. There's a decency in you, a goodness that makes you seek out people in need, instead of turning your back on them. Like your kids. Like the dogs. Hell, even like that sorry rooster who won't make a sound." He lifted one hand to her cheek and brushed her flushed skin with a profound reverence. "You don't need all those bottles and jars, Sarah. Your beauty shines out from inside you."

He watched as wariness and trust vied with each other in the depths of her remarkable eyes. It had been a long, long time since anyone had had faith in him. Suddenly, he needed Sarah's faith the way he needed his next breath.

Trust me, he willed silently. I need you to believe in me. The doorbell rang.

"Damn," Sarah said, "I forgot that Mrs. Perkins was coming over. She'll talk for hours."

"Let it ring," Luke said.

"I can't. She was Aunt Connie's best friend, practically family."

She pulled away from Luke before he could stop her. The doorbell rang again, and she hurried to answer it. But as she left, she paused and glanced back at him with a haunted expression. "I just . . . can't," she said, her hushed voice indicating that she was answering an entirely different question. Then she was gone.

Luke stared at the empty doorway, consigning Mrs. Perkins to the devil. He'd been so close to breaking down Sarah's defenses and winning her trust. He shook his head in profound consternation. As he did, he caught sight of his reflection in the mirror over the bathroom sink.

An outlaw looked back at him. Luke stared at the disreputable character, at his shaggy, sun-streaked hair, desperate eyes, and a face that could make even a stretch of unpaved highway look good. He rubbed his shadowed chin and felt the uneven rasp of beard stubble. Hell, no wonder she'd run.

Bone-deep weariness settled around him like a shroud. He bent down and picked up the discarded wrench and resumed work on the sink. Of course she didn't trust him. The lady had brains as well as beauty. She was too smart by half to waste her time on a weathered strip of rawhide like him. Hell, nothing could come of it anyway. A month of civilization couldn't wipe out ten years of living like a renegade.

He was a fool to wish it could.

They'd gotten the saying wrong, Sarah thought, as she watched Luke stalk across the night-shadowed yard toward the tack room. It should be "Hell hath no fury like a *man* scorned." Ever since the plumbing incident two days before, he'd behaved like an injured grizzly bear. And she hadn't behaved much better.

Sarah turned away from the window and tried to concentrate on drying the last of the supper dishes, but Luke's image haunted her. She recalled in every detail the gentle strength of his hands on her shoulders, the rough, seductive timbre of his voice, the unmistakable gleam of desire in his eyes. Desire for her. *You don't need all those bottles and jars, Sarah. Your beauty shines out from inside you.*

She twisted the dishtowel into a tortured spiral. "It's physical, only physical," she muttered, repeating the words that were quickly becoming her personal mantra. It had to be. She'd examined the facts with legal detachment, concluding that Luke was attracted to her only because he was a virile male animal and she was the sole woman within reach. Not very flattering, but it fit the facts. Luke's desire for her had more to do with hormones than hearts. After he left Corners, he'd forget about her in a week. And she would forget about him just as quickly.

And pigs will fly. . . .

She threw the towel aside and stripped off her apron, angry at fate, the building inspector, and anyone else who might have conspired to bring Luke Tyrell into her perfectly happy life. She'd been doing fine until he came along. Well, maybe not all that fine. She couldn't have made the repairs without his help. And, although she dearly loved her children, there were times when loneliness welled up inside her so strong, she thought she'd choke on it. She hadn't felt lonely once since he'd arrived. At least, not until two days ago.

Belatedly, Sarah realized how much she'd come to depend on Luke. He knew more about farming than all her agricultural books and pamphlets combined, and she'd come to rely on his thoughtful advice. They'd worked well together, their individual strengths and weaknesses meshing like a fine-tuned machine. Sarah had the vision, and Luke had the strength and knowledge to make it real.

But more than anything else, she missed the quiet times they'd shared. Often, after a long, exhausting day of work, they'd sit beside each other on the porch, just listening to the sounds of the night. Sarah had never known such peace in a man's presence, and she cherished every moment of it.

Those days were gone for good, she realized bleakly. All because of a plastic dinosaur, a jar of face cream, and a mysterious woman named Annie . . .

Micah barreled into the kitchen, interrupting her thoughts. "Valerie's bitching again."

"Complaining, Micah," Sarah said sternly. His statement was hardly a news flash. Valerie had been in bed with a sore throat all day, and she had been *complaining* them to death. Micah was the only one besides Sarah still paying attention to her, and that was because he was half-hoping her disease would turn into something more medically interesting.

"I'd better go up and see her," Sarah said as she hung up her apron and headed for the door.

"Oh, you don't have to. I already got Luke."

Sarah stopped midstep. "Luke?"

"Yeah. Valerie asked for him, so I went out to the barn and got him. He's up with her now."

Good Lord, Sarah thought. The grizzly and the whiner. She raced up the back stairs, ready to break up what promised to be a very ugly scene. She was almost at Valerie's door before it struck her that Luke had voluntarily left the barn and come all the way back to the house to see a sick child. For the second time in as many minutes she stopped in her tracks.

Then she heard the sound of Valerie's laughter.

"Do it again," her daughter said between giggles.

Sarah heard a deep huff of exasperation. "I've already done it twice, little bit."

Little bit? Sarah didn't know which stunned her more—Luke's use of the pet name or the unfamiliar warmth in his tone. She crept closer and peered through the partially open door.

Valerie sat propped against her pillows, clutching her beloved Mr. Bear to her chest. Luke sat on the other end of her bed. The hard-bitten cowboy looked surprisingly at home propped on the edge of Valerie's pink down comforter. Sarah couldn't help remembering the first night, when he'd yelled at the girl and frightened her half to death. Now they shared smiles and laughter like the best of friends. Could a man change so much in a month?

The lamp on the bedside table backlighted Luke's profile, softening his hard features with a sunset glow. Sarah had never seen him look more at ease. Or more handsome. A strange, hopeless hunger began to gnaw at her. She wanted . . . she needed . . .

"Please, just once more," Valerie said, sounding tragic.

Luke's austere mouth curled into a gentle smile. "Okay. But this is the *last* time." He cleared his throat, then began singing the theme song from "The Flintstones" in a low, decidedly off-key baritone.

Sarah slipped away from the door, biting her lip to keep from crying aloud. Wanting ripped through her like a violent wind. Maelstroms of fire coursed through her, burning away the tall, restrictive walls she'd built around herself to keep the world at a safe distance. And when the burning was done, she sagged against the wall, weak and exhausted. And free.

Unafraid, she faced the truth she'd been denying for days, maybe weeks. She wasn't shallowly attracted to Luke. She was in love with him. Every cell in her body blazed with love for him. Her weariness dissipated like morning fog in sunshine. She looked around, amazed that the world hadn't split apart from the force of the miracle that had taken place inside her. A moment ago she'd been dead to all feelings. Loving Luke had brought her back to life.

She heard a sound behind her. Turning, she saw that Luke had left Valerie's room. She watched as he quietly closed the door, then started down the hallway toward her. Distracted by his own private thoughts, he walked past without seeing her.

"Luke," she whispered. She'd wanted to shout his name, but a whisper was all she could manage.

He spun around. For a scant moment she saw the afterglow of the warmth he'd felt for Valerie shining in his eyes. Then the familiar icy defensiveness hardened his expression. "Well? What do you want?"

Sarah almost winced as the harsh words hit her sensitive ears. But she didn't back down. She opened her mouth, wanting to thank him for reminding her that love existed and that she was still capable of feeling it. But the words wouldn't come. Too late, she realized there weren't any words for the tremendous emotions inside her. Joy couldn't be measured in sound bites. Love couldn't be squeezed into four ordinary letters. She opened her mouth again, but still no words came. She only felt helpless and inadequate, and more than a little foolish.

Luke said nothing. He watched her eyes, studying the complex emotions mirrored in her gaze. Then, without any hesitation, he cupped her face in his big, callused hands and lowered his lips to hers.

SEVEN

The man could kiss. His mouth covered hers with devastating gentleness, moving across hers with a moist, warm, and very thorough caress. His knowing tongue skimmed her lips playfully, driving her mad with promises. Tiny shock waves of pleasure rippled through her arms and midsection, arousing her more than she would have believed possible from a single kiss. But Luke made miracles happen inside her. When he captured her lower lip with his teeth and tugged on her sensitive flesh, she shuddered.

"Sarah," he murmured against her lips.

He spoke her name softly, like a prayer, but there was nothing religious about the way it made her feel. The tremors inside her turned to earthquakes, shaking her to her vulnerable core. Heat shimmered up her legs and pooled in her abdomen, thrilling and frightening her at once. Common sense advised her to pull away, but her body had a will of its own. Heedless of the warning, she tilted back her head to allow him easier access.

He accepted her unspoken invitation. Sliding his hands to her shoulders, he seared a trail of hot kisses across her cheek and down the side of her throat. She heard him whisper something about her ear, then felt him nibbling her sensitive lobe. Fire erupted through her. She loved him and yearned to feel his lips on other vulnerable parts of her body, but she vaguely remembered there was some reason she shouldn't be doing this. An important reason.

She opened her mouth to ask him to stop and immediately found herself in the midst of a deeper, wetter, and even more serious kiss. His tongue delved between her parted lips and explored her mouth's softness with an erotic experience that turned her knees to jelly. Yet his kiss was still tender, giving her pleasure as well as taking it. She placed her open palms on his chest, intending to push him away. Instead, her traitorous fingers caressed his neck and shoulders.

"Sarah," he repeated. His voice was rough and urgent. His arms tightened around her, crushing her against his broad chest.

Heat and life coursed through her, searing her senses in a maelstrom of fire. The censuring voice inside her died, silenced by her overpowering need. She wanted this, this feel of Luke's strong arms around her, this sweet, killing fire. Eagerly, she nestled closer and ravaged his mouth with the hunger of a body starved too long for physical loving. She tasted him deeply, reveling in the pure sensuality of exploring him, loving the strength, the heat, the reality of him. Loving him.

Then, unexpectedly, he stopped. He lifted his head, his eyes still glazed with desire, and gently untangled their arms and bodies. He stepped away from her, ignoring the soft mew of protest from her unsatisfied lips. She blinked in bewilderment, confused and disoriented by the sudden loss of his heat. Then she heard the sound of small footsteps pounding up the stairs behind her. A moment later Micah appeared on the landing, looking winded and anxious.

"Sarah, you gotta come quick," he said breathlessly. "Rafe and Jenny are fighting again. I think they're going to kill each other!"

Feeling breathless herself, Sarah was sorely tempted to tell Micah to let them. She glanced at Luke, wondering if he regretted the interruption half as much as she did. As usual, his impassive face gave nothing away. "I . . . I guess I'd better go break up the fight," she said, feeling more awkward than she ever had in her life. She had a million things she wanted to say to Luke, not one of which could be said in front of Micah. "Thank you, Luke . . . for coming to see Valerie."

His expression didn't change a whisker, but a deep, burnished humor rumbled in his voice. "My pleasure, ma'am."

Later, after punishments had been assigned and

the kids were in bed, Sarah sat in the dark in her room and relived the glory of Luke's kiss. She drew her knees up under her chin and locked her arms around them, grinning like a schoolgirl in the throes of her first crush. She felt giddy and light-headed. She blushed every other minute—it was hard not to when she remembered the shameless intimacy of Luke's caress and her equally shameless response. If Micah hadn't shown up when he did, she would have given herself to Luke right then and there. And she wouldn't have regretted it for a second.

She'd never imagined she could feel this fire, this delight with a man. Love put an extra spin on things. The hard-edged loner who'd blown into her life like a tumbleweed had taken root in her heart. She wanted to please him in every way a woman could please a man. She wanted to listen to his dreams and tell him hers and forge a future out of their melded dreams. But most of all she wanted like hell to kiss him again, and not just on his lips.

She blushed again at the blatantly lustful direction of her thoughts. She'd always been so sensible, so rational, about sex—until she'd felt Luke's mouth cover hers. Sensible had flown out the window. She brushed her fingers across her still-tender lips, remembering the heat, the roughness, the taste of him. Her breath quickened, and an aching sweetness throbbed deep within her. She'd never felt this primitive hunger for a man. She'd certainly never felt this way about any of her recent dates. Why, not even when she was married to Paul—

Paul.

Her smile died. *Don't remember!* she told herself, but the painful memories invaded her mind all the same. Blizzard-cold, they sapped the warmth and joy from her heart.

She'd married Paul just after they'd graduated from law school, when they were both idealistic young attorneys eager to save the world. Originally, they'd both wanted to adopt unwanted children to give the kids a chance in life, but Paul's interest in the idea had dwindled as his political aspirations grew. He ran for the city council on a platform of helping the underprivileged, but he planned to accomplish this by creating new programs, all high-level and impersonal. Sarah became concerned, worried that he was distancing himself from the real needs and problems of the community. She wanted to talk to him about it, but he was too busy with the campaign, spending almost every waking minute with the members of his staff, especially with his personal aide Mallory.

Sarah found out about their affair a month before the election. Hurt and betrayed, she'd confronted him, but he'd assured her that Mallory meant nothing to him and begged her not to leave. Sarah wasn't a quitter. She'd agreed to stay with him and to give their marriage another chance. A month later Paul was elected to the city council.

The room's darkness closed in around her as she remembered the last months of her marriage. Paul had promised her time and time again that his affair with Mallory was over, and that he wanted to make their marriage work as much as she did. Yet all the while he was seeing Mallory behind her back.

Hot tears stung Sarah's eyes. One night Paul had asked her to come home early from work to discuss something important. He'd come in a drink or two past sober and bluntly announced that he was moving out. He told her that he'd always care about her in a special way, but that it was Mallory he loved. Perfect, politically correct Mallory.

Sarah knew Paul hadn't set out to hurt her, but that didn't change the fact that he'd torn her apart. And if she'd hurt that much over Paul, how would she be able to bear it if Luke went back to Annie?

Sarah had heard the longing in Luke's voice when he'd cried out Annie's name. He still loved her—so much so that he couldn't even bear to have her name spoken aloud. Grief and envy vied in Sarah's heart. Luke might accept her love and even appear to return it, but eventually he would leave her and go back to the woman he truly loved . . . as Paul had left her for Mallory.

There was only one thing to do. Ruthlessly, Sarah rubbed away her tears, determined not to make a fool of herself a second time. She'd fallen in love with Luke Tyrell. She'd just have to make herself fall out of love with him.

Yet even as the thought crossed her mind, she realized how absurd it was. She loved Luke in a way she had never loved Paul, not even in the early days of their courtship. Loving Luke had changed her. He was as much a part of her as her breath and her blood. She might as well ask her heart to stop beating as to tell herself to stop loving Luke. She crawled under her covers, wondering when the night had become so cold and lonely.

"It's not fair," she said into the silence.

Fair is where you take your hog to win blue ribbons.

For once her aunt's words didn't bring her a smile or a bit of comfort.

"The bacon's burning!"

Jenny's cry startled Sarah out of her thoughts. She pulled the smoking pan off the burner, silently cursing herself for her foolishness. Damn, couldn't she keep her mind off Luke long enough to get her children fed and off to school?

Sarah drained the bacon and served it up to her kids with eggs and a basket of hot biscuits. They emptied both their plates and the basket at light speed. Sarah refilled the basket and shook her head, wondering if they even tasted the food they scarfed down. Smiling at their more than healthy appetites as they helped themselves to more biscuits, she removed the empty platters and carried them to the sink.

Suddenly, Lyn appeared at her side. "Are you okay?" the oldest girl asked in her low, melodious voice.

"I didn't get much sleep last night," Sarah hedged. Actually, she hadn't gotten *any* sleep. She'd spent the better part of the night worrying about how she was going to face Luke this morning. When she'd finally worked up enough courage to come downstairs, she'd found a note tacked to the back door saying he'd gone to check the pasture fence and would be late for breakfast. Waiting was going to drive her crazy.

Sarah felt the butterfly brush of Lyn's hand on her arm. "I can stay home if you want. . . ."

Sarah looked down into her daughter's cornflower-blue eyes. Unlike her other children, Lyn had never told Sarah much about her background, and her case file had been sketchy. Still, Sarah had seen enough abuse cases to guess that Lyn had been through something pretty traumatic—something that had made her wary and wise beyond her years. Lyn had the maturity to understand Sarah's complex feelings for Luke, and it would be easier for Sarah to face him if Lyn stayed.

For a moment Sarah was tempted, but her kids had been through enough. She would face down an army of Lukes before she'd use one of her children as an emotional shield. She covered Lyn's hand and gave it a reassuring squeeze. "If I were you, I'd worry about something important, like how you're going to keep Jenny and Rafe from starting a fight on the school bus."

"I never start fights!" cried Jenny and Rafe in unison. Glaring at each other, they opened their mouths to continue, but the sharp blast of the school-bus horn silenced their argument.

Half a whirlwind minute later, the kids had grabbed their lunches and left the house, banging the screen door behind them. Sarah leaned back against the counter and closed her eyes, savoring the blissful moment of complete silence, but before she could get used to it, she heard the back door squeak open. *Rafe must have forgotten his homework again*, she thought, as she reluctantly opened her eyes.

It wasn't Rafe. Luke stood by the door, rugged, windblown, and so handsome, it stopped her breath. He wasn't looking at her, but instead concentrated on stripping a pair of heavy work gloves from his hands. He roughly pulled them off and set them on the table beside his Stetson. Each unhurried movement echoed through her, arousing her in an instant until her whole body screamed for his touch. *My God, he hasn't even looked at me yet. . . .*

Sarah cleared her throat, determined to keep her wits about her. "Good morning, Luke. I wanted to talk to you about—"

She got no further. With the same unhurried ease Luke had used to remove his gloves, he reached out and folded her into his arms and gave her a sensual, consuming kiss. Ecstasy engulfed her, turning her blood to fire and her bones to water. When he released her, she had to grip the counter for support.

" 'Morning," he said pleasantly as he swung his leg over one of the chairs and sat down at the table. "What's for breakfast?"

Sarah swallowed, valiantly trying to rein in her stampeding senses. Public speaking had once been her stock-in-trade, but at the moment she could barely remember how to string two words together. "Luke. Last night. The . . . kiss." She took a steadying breath before she continued. "It can't happen again."

Luke shrugged and reached for a biscuit. "Just did," he commented. "Got any jam?"

Sarah closed her eyes and fought an almost unbearable ache of love for him. He looked so content, so completely happy. She wished she could give him jam and kisses and whatever else he needed to bring that rare, sweet smile to his hardened features. It would be so easy to give in to her love for him . . . and so destructive. Remember Annie, her inner voice cautioned. And Mallory.

She opened her eyes, drawing bitter strength from her cold core of memories. "A relationship between us couldn't possibly work, Luke. We're too different."

Luke's hand stilled above the biscuits. "Different?"

"We have nothing in common," she continued, rushing to get the words of her rehearsed speech out before she lost her resolve. "You're from the country. I'm from the city. We've got different backgrounds, different goals. We want different things out of life." Silently, she added, *I want you, but you want Annie.*

Luke's eyes narrowed. "You didn't seem to give a damn about our differences a minute ago."

She heard the harsh edge in his voice and knew he was hurting. More than anything she wanted to reach out and soothe the deep scowl lines on his face, to kiss away the tightness around his mouth. But she knew that could lead only to more heartache, more despair. She couldn't bear to go through the torment again, not with him. Better to make the break now, before she became too involved. *Right,* her conscience chided, *like before you fall in love with him.*

She turned to the sink, knowing she couldn't face him and say what needed to be said. "I don't want you to kiss me again. I . . . I can't make it any clearer than that."

"No, you sure can't make it clearer. You're the boss, and I'm the hired help." His bitter words smashing the crystal silence like a fist through a mirror. "I'd best learn to keep my place."

Sarah whirled around. "That's not what I meant."

"The hell it isn't." He shoved back his chair, the sharp movement making an ugly grating sound against the kitchen floor. He bolted to his feet, grabbed up his hat and work gloves, and stalked to the door.

"Wait," she cried. "Let me explain—"

Before she could finish the sentence, he'd slammed the door behind him.

Sarah bit her lip, giving in to the tears she knew she didn't have a prayer of stopping. *I did the right thing*, she told herself. *I did the only thing I could do*.

So why did she feel as if she'd nailed the lid on her own coffin?

Thunk.

Luke stilled his hammer blows and pulled the red bandanna out of his back pocket, wiping the sweat from his brow. Sinking fence posts was a hard, dirty job, but he welcomed the grueling task. It took his mind off Sarah. Sort of.

"Different," he muttered as he stuffed the bandanna back into his pocket. "Goals and backgrounds. Like hell."

All around him the resplendent Texas sun poured its brilliance on the waiting land, but Luke was blind to its glory. Day or night, it mattered little. He carried the darkness inside him and an icy emptiness that couldn't be touched by the sun. Only a kiss could warm him. Sarah's kiss.

Last night when he'd held her in his arms, he'd felt as if he'd been given a priceless gift. He'd kissed his share of women in his time, but none had ever affected him like Sarah. Her caresses had reached inside him, soothing his deep wounds like a sweet, healing balm. He'd felt all the broken pieces of his life come back together, then fuse from the heat of her guileless passion. She'd been so innocent, so giving . . . and so damn explosive it nearly took the top of his head off. He'd fallen asleep with a smile on his lips, believing there still might be things in the world like hope, and dreams, and second chances.

And proved himself to be the biggest fool this side of El Paso.

"Different." His tone made the word a curse. He positioned the fence post and brought the hammer down with a satisfying thud. Miss Citified Ex-lawyer might think she was something special, but he'd like to see her try to sink this fence post on her own. She needed him to do her dirty work for her. And, whether she admitted it or not, she needed other things from him as well.

A glint of metal caught his eye. Bending down, he picked up a slim-bladed pocketknife that had been half-embedded in the ground. It was an expensive item, the kind made more for show than use. Its blade had been cruelly blunted. Luke turned the ruined knife over in his hand, a dark suspicion forming in his mind. He'd noticed the post needed replacing when he'd come out to repair the fence's broken barbwire. Now he wondered if the rusted wire hadn't been helped along a bit by this knife's owner.

He considered telling Sarah but almost immediately decided against it. The knife could have been dropped months ago. It was hardly proof of vandalism. Besides, if he did tell her, she might go all scared and weepy, and he'd have to handle the whole thing on his own anyway. Not that the idea of comforting a distraught Sarah didn't hold a certain appeal. . . .

Damn! He was *supposed* to be angry with her. He gave the post an extra pound, then scooped up his hat and headed back across the pasture. He passed Sarah's "herd" on the way out, but neither of the steers bothered to lift its head, apparently more interested in hay than in him. Luke smiled grimly, feeling a measure of envy. Give the cattle a trough of water and a hearty meal, and they were perfectly content. If only his life could be so easy.

He passed by the steers, giving the nearest one a pat on the flank. "Take my advice, fella. Don't ever get mixed up with a woman."

MacNeil—or was it Lehrer?—raised his head and eyed Luke with a fathomless bovine stare. He stopped and tipped back his hat, wondering whether he was looking at the wisest or the dumbest beast in the world. Nope, not the dumbest. He reserved that spot for himself.

He'd let a woman get under his skin, something he'd sworn he'd never do again. He'd let himself want her. And the worst of it was, he still did. Wanting her was twisting his insides. He wanted her even after that condemning speech in the kitchen. Even after he knew she considered him beneath her, a charity case like the rest of her strays.

Well, he wasn't a stray, and he'd be damned before he'd let her treat him like one. He was a man, with a man's desires, and what he desired at the moment was Sarah in his bed. And, judging by that hellfire kiss she'd given him, it was exactly what she wanted too. He'd gotten to her, differences or no differences.

Luke pulled his hat back down over his brow, smiling grimly at the contrariness of life. All over Texas there were women waiting to welcome him into their arms, but the one he wanted wouldn't give him the time of day. But, hell, maybe it was for the best. Sarah was the kind of woman who would want more from him than a purely physical relationship— and that was the only kind of relationship he was prepared to offer. Love was a fairy tale he'd stopped believing in a long time ago. And dreams could kill a man faster than cheap whiskey and bad women.

EIGHT

"School bus!"

Sarah's kitchen was suddenly filled with five small whirling dervishes who grabbed books, homework, and lunches as they headed for the door. Five separate shouts of "Good-bye, Sarah!" were followed by four separate bangs of the screen door slamming shut. Sarah, engaged in trying to fit one more item into her overstuffed refrigerator, waited for the final slam. It didn't come.

She stilled, her skin growing hot despite the refrigerator's coolness. She lifted her head, knowing whom she would see standing in the doorway.

"Morning," he said gruffly.

He tossed his work gloves on the table and headed for the coffeepot, barely sparing a look in her direction. It didn't surprise her. Since their confrontation four days before, he'd spoken maybe a dozen words to her, all of them surly. She should have gotten used to his curtness by now, but she hadn't. Not by a long shot.

"Good morning," she replied, using her forced smile to hide her pain. "I hope you slept well."

He shrugged, apparently far more interested in her coffee than in her. "Storm's coming. I'll check the drainage ditches, then finish as much of the roof as I can before it rains."

Sarah looked out the window at the gray smudge forming on the horizon. They had four hours, maybe five. "That's a lot to do in a few hours. Maybe I could work on the roof while—"

"No." His stone-hard word crushed her good intentions. "Roofing's a man's job. If you need something to do, you can patch the chicken wire on the coop."

If you need something to do. Sarah bit her lip, stifling the dual ache of anger and disappointment. He used to value her help. They'd worked as a team, her attention to detail perfectly complementing his skill and strength. Now he barely tolerated her assistance. It wasn't fair. So much of what had happened between them wasn't fair.

"Luke?"

He glanced at her, his eyes dark and unreadable. "What?"

Sarah drew a deep breath. Wisdom urged her to keep her mouth shut. Desperation made her bold. "I know we haven't been on the best terms lately, but . . . well, we used to be friends. I miss it. I miss talking to you, joking with you, even arguing with you. I miss asking you about the farm, and I miss having you tell me what a damn fool I was for taking on Corners in the first place. Can't we at least try to be friends again?"

At first he didn't answer. He refilled his coffee cup and took a long, slow sip, as if he hadn't heard her. His chiseled features remained impassive, as harshly remote as a granite cliff face. Sarah swallowed, wondering if he was going to ignore her again, and wondering how she would bear it. The bright kitchen suddenly seemed like a tomb.

Then he spoke, his words cutting the silence like the edge of an old, rusty knife. "What about all our *differences*? I'm only the hired hand, remember?"

"I never said that. I never even meant that."

He lifted his gaze, riveting her with his fierce, unforgiving stare. "Then what, exactly, did you mean?"

She opened her mouth, then closed it again without a word. What could she say? If she explained her fears about Annie, she'd have to tell him everything about her painful history with Paul and Mallory. Sarah was no coward, but she knew she wasn't brave enough to face all her demons at once. "You'll have to trust me."

Luke's harsh laugh grated against her ears. "Like hell. The only thing I have to do is finish repairing this sorry place so I can head on to Houston."

He drained his mug, then slammed it down on

the counter hard enough to set her teeth on edge. He stalked toward the door, grabbing up his work gloves from the table as he passed. Sarah groaned, cursing herself for making a bad situation even worse. "Luke, wait—"

Her words were drowned out by the slamming door.

Dammit, she thought, as she watched him through the window. "He can go clear ditches," she stated aloud. "He can go to hell for all I care."

Later, she continued the conversation in the same vein with Cogburn the rooster. "He's arrogant, bad-tempered, and rude," she told her feathered confessor as she stood in front of the coop and measured out a length of chicken wire. "And he's got a chip on his shoulder as wide as the Brazos. No woman in her right mind would have anything to do with him."

Cogburn eyed her from his perch on the fence post, tilting his head in unblinking avian condemnation.

"Don't you start with me," she warned. "You men always stick together. The truth is, we'll be better off without him—"

A distant peal of thunder interrupted her. She looked up and saw a bank of angry thunderheads massing on the horizon. Nasty, she thought. I hope Luke comes back soon. Then she remembered that she wasn't supposed to care what happened to him.

Trouble was, she cared with all her heart.

The inspection was only three weeks away. She

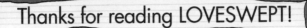

Thanks for reading LOVESWEPT!

Now, enter our

Winners Classic
SWEEPSTAKES
and go for the
Vacation Of Your Dreams!

Here's your chance to win a *fabulous* 14-day holiday for two in romantic Hawaii ... exciting Europe ... or the sizzling Caribbean! Use one of these stickers to tell us your choice — and *go for it!*

Plus —
$5,000⁰⁰
CASH!

 Send Me To
HAWAII

 Send Me To
EUROPE

Send Me
To The
CARIBBEAN

 Send My
FREE
BOOKS!

**6
FREE
BOOKS!**

Six scintillating
Loveswept romance novels
and a chance to win the vacation of
your dreams — are YOURS FREE!

NO COST OR OBLIGATION TO BUY
See details inside ...

Ah, Romance...

Don't you just *love* being in love? And what could be
more romantic than you and your special someone sunning
on the beach in exotic Hawaii, holding hands, listening to the
pounding surf ... or strolling arm and arm around London,
hearing Big Ben strike midnight as you toast each other with
champagne ... or slipping out of a casino to walk along the silky
beaches of the Caribbean on a warm, moonlit night?
Sounds wonderful, doesn't it?

WIN A ROMANTIC INTERLUDE AND $5,000.00 CASH!

What's even *more* wonderful is that **you could win** one of these
romantic **14-day vacations for two**, plus **$5,000.00 CASH**,
in the Winners Classic Sweepstakes! To enter, just affix the vacation
sticker of your choice to your Official Entry Form and drop it in the mail.
It costs you nothing to enter (we even pay postage!) — so ***go for it!***

FREE GIFTS!

We've got **six FREE Loveswept Romances** ready to send you, too!

If you affix the FREE BOOKS sticker to your Entry Form, your first
shipment of Loveswept Romances is yours absolutely FREE. Plus, about
once a month, you'll get six *new* books hot off the presses, *before they're
available in bookstores.* You'll always have 15 days to decide whether to
keep any shipment, for our low regular price, currently just $13.50* —
that's 6 books for the price of four! **You are never obligated to keep
any shipment**, and may cancel at any time by writing "cancel" across our
invoice and returning the shipment to us, at our expense. There's **no risk**
and **no obligation** to buy, *ever.*

**SIX LOVESWEPT ROMANCES ARE ABSOLUTELY FREE AND ARE
YOURS TO KEEP FOREVER,** no matter what you decide about future
shipments! So come on! You risk nothing at all — and you stand to gain
a world of sizzling romance, exciting prizes ... and FREE LOVESWEPTS!

*(plus shipping & handling, and sales tax in NY and Canada)

needed to keep her mind focused on finishing the necessary repairs, yet all too often she found herself consumed by thoughts of Luke. Part of her wanted to throttle him for his surliness. Part of her burned with guilt because she'd helped to cause the hurt his surliness masked. Her need to strangle him was almost as powerful as her need to comfort him, and the combination was tearing her apart. She couldn't eat for worrying about him, and she couldn't sleep for fear she'd dream about him. Most of all, she wondered how she was going to be able to bear it after he went away. . . .

A strong gust of wind blew through the yard and knocked the pompous Cogburn off his commanding position on the fence post. Sarah grinned as she watched the rooster flap his feathers, trying to recover both his perch and his dignity. She was about to reach out and offer the bird a helping hand when another flapping sound caught her attention.

She glanced up toward the direction of the sound— her barn's roof. Luke had started to fix the damaged section and had covered his half-finished work with a tarpaulin. But the storm's rising wind had ripped part of the tarp free of its moorings. Now it flapped loudly against the roof, exposing the unprotected section to the fury of the coming storm.

The tarp had to be secured before the storm came. If it wasn't, Luke would have to re-paper the area and lose several days' work in the process. Cogburn's coop would have to wait, Sarah thought, as she put aside the chicken wire. She hurried across the yard, intending to find Luke and have him fix the roof, but her steps slowed as she passed the ladder set against the barn.

The storm was rising quickly. She could smell the edge of it in the air and taste the building humidity on her tongue. She wouldn't have time to track down Luke and bring him back before the storm arrived. The work on the roof was sure to suffer, unless she went up and secured the tarp herself.

Sarah raised her eyes to the long, straight length of the ladder. A knot of anxiety formed in her stomach. She wasn't afraid of heights, but she had a healthy respect for them, and she didn't welcome the idea of climbing over a pitched roof in a rising wind. Luke had forbidden her to set one foot on the ladder, claiming it was too dangerous for a woman, but since repairing the roof was essential to passing the county inspection, she didn't feel she had much choice.

Resolved, she climbed the tall ladder. The wind plastered her shirt against her body and sent strands of hair whipping across her cheeks. Fighting the force of the wind, Sarah cautiously worked her way across the roof to the tarp moorings and grabbed hold of the lines. The coarse rope stung her hands, and the gusting wind filled the heavy material like a sail, painfully wrenching her shoulders as she tried to control it, but eventually she was able to secure the tarp back in place. She tied the mooring lines, knotting them so tightly that nothing short of a tornado could pull them free. Exhausted but satisfied, she pushed her wind-tangled hair out of her face and started back to the ladder.

A sudden gust of wind blew her hair into her eyes. Momentarily blinded, Sarah missed her footing. She slipped and slid down the pitched side of the roof, fighting for a handhold but finding none. She plunged right to the edge before her foot hit a level place between the roof and one of the wooden mooring blocks. Unfortunately, the force of her descent wedged her foot tightly between the block and the roof. She couldn't gain enough leverage on the steep surface to pull herself free.

Sarah's courtroom training had taught her how to keep a cool head in a crisis. She gritted her teeth and tried to keep her wits about her, even when the first fat drops of rain began to fall. She was safe for the moment, ironically secured to the roof by the same mooring as the tarpaulin. Eventually, Luke would come back from his work in the fields and save her. If he saw her . . .

She closed her eyes, fighting a wave of panic. She couldn't die, not yet. Her farm needed her. Her kids needed her. And, although she'd been afraid to face it until this moment, she knew that Luke, too, needed her. Regret stabbed through her. Luke had reached out to her, and she'd retreated, frightened by the memory of her past. She'd denied the truest, deepest feeling she'd ever had for a stupid memory of a man she no longer loved. *Sarah, you've done some dumb things in your life, but this tops them all!*

She wouldn't make that mistake again. Life was too short to waste on regrets. The next time she saw Luke, she was going to tell him how she felt about him, and damn the consequences.

A sudden bolt of lightning speared down from the sky. *If there is a next time*, she amended.

Rain, Luke decided as he shouldered his pitchfork and headed back across the fields, could be damn inconvenient. He'd lose hours to this storm, maybe the entire afternoon. It irked him, even though in truth his body couldn't have taken much more of the abuse he'd been giving it. He'd ripped out three days' worth of ditch weeds in three hours' time, and his muscles burned from the effort. Still, he welcomed the backbreaking work because it kept his mind off Sarah.

Can't we at least try to be friends?

Her words echoed through his mind, damning him with their simple honesty. He had been treating her badly, punishing her for rejecting him. But, dammit, that was her choice. Sulking about her decision was a childish, cowardly thing to do, and he was heartily ashamed of his actions. Besides, he missed their friendship too. Almost as much as he missed kissing her.

He turned his face to the sky, ignoring the soft rain that pattered his face. "All right," he muttered, "I will try to be just friends. It'll probably kill me, but I'll try. Satisfied?"

Stronger, wetter raindrops were his only answer.

Sighing, he swung the pitchfork to his other shoulder, distributing the weight among his tortured muscles. But the pain in his body was nothing compared to the pain in his heart. Since Annie's death he'd kept women at a distance. He'd built a high fortress around himself to protect him from another relationship and the inevitable pain that would come with it. He thought he'd done a damn fine job, too, until Sarah's sweet kiss crumbled those walls into a mountain of rubble. Dammit, couldn't she see how special it was between them? If she took off her big-city blinders for a moment and looked, really looked, at him, she'd see—

She'd see a broken-down cowboy with a bad reputation and a bleak future, his conscience chided. It was the truth. Sarah was a fine, decent woman, and she deserved a fine, decent man. Luke had misplaced both those virtues years ago.

A conscience, he realized glumly, could be as damned inconvenient as the rain.

A streak of lightning blazed across the sky, illuminating the field, the house, the barn. . . . Luke halted, stunned by what the burst of light had momentarily revealed. Narrowing his eyes, he peered upward through the curtain of rain to the now-shadowed roof. For a moment he'd thought he'd seen . . . No. It couldn't be.

Another lightning flash showed him it *was*.

Luke threw down the pitchfork and started across

the field at a dead run. The soggy ground fought him every step of the way, tormenting his already overworked muscles. He hardly noticed the pain. All his thoughts were focused on the fragile body he'd seen clinging to the barn's high roof.

Not again. Please, God, not again!

"Hold on," he yelled. He was too far away for her to hear, but he yelled anyway. "Sarah, hold on!"

Precious minutes passed before he reached the ladder, and more as he climbed to the top. The rain fell in thick sheets now, obscuring his vision. Hell and damnation, why had Sarah come up here? Once he got her to safety, he was going to give her the tongue-lashing of her life. *If he got her to safety*.

"Over here."

Luke turned, uncertain whether the faint sound had been Sarah's voice or his own wishful thinking. Trusting his instincts, he stumbled toward the sound, slipping and sliding on the roof's pitched tiles.

"Be careful," she called.

Luke gave a shout of relieved laughter. It wasn't his imagination—only Sarah could be crazy and caring enough to warn *him* to be careful when she was the one in trouble. He made his way toward her, half walking, half crawling across the rain-slick surface. He came upon her so suddenly that he almost tripped over her.

She looked at him, her eyes shining with confidence and trust. "I knew you'd come."

Briefly, he let himself believe he was the man she

thought he was. Her faith made him a king. Pride swelled him. He'd have fought lions for her at that moment. He bent down and started to lift her.

"Wait. My foot's caught by the wood block," she protested. "You'll have to get a crowbar to—"

Before she could say another word, Luke brought his booted foot squarely down on the offending block, knocking it into oblivion. With her support gone she started to slip, but Luke's strong arms held her fast, saving her from falling. Although she didn't cry out, she clung to him like a drowning woman to a life raft, her actions betraying her fear. Truthfully, Luke was almost as scared as Sarah, but he'd have died before he'd let her know it. For once in his life he was going to be the hero she needed.

Holding her tight against him, he scooted over the treacherous roof. Thunder roared. Almost at the same instant lightning struck nearby. Sarah froze and cried out in panic. Luke cradled her against him, whispering words of comfort in her ear. Gradually, her body relaxed, and he gently urged her forward, a few inches at a time.

Somehow they made it to the ladder and safely down to the ground. The second her feet touched solid earth, Sarah's strength deserted her. She sagged against him, exhausted by fear and exposure. He lifted her up and carried her out of the rain and into the barn, setting her down on a soft pile of straw in an empty stall. He knelt down beside her and smoothed back her damp, heavy hair. "Are you all right?"

She thought a moment, then nodded.

"Good. So maybe you could tell me what the hell you were doing up there."

"Fixing the tarp. The wind blew it loose, and I went up to secure it."

"With a storm coming?" he demanded, his bottled-up fear finally rising to the surface.

"That's why I had to do it. The rain would have ruined all the work you'd done on the roof, and I—"

"Who cares about the damn roof?" He started to pace the stall, angrily shoving his fingers through his rain-soaked hair. "Of all the brainless, reckless things to do. Damn, Sarah, even your cows have more sense than that!"

"Don't yell at me," she warned, her own temper rising. "I was only trying to help."

"You almost helped yourself into an early grave!" He turned to the open barn door and stared out into the full fury of the storm, his hands curling into fists. "Dammit, Sarah, I've already lost someone I cared about in an accident. I don't think I could stand losing you too."

The storm winds blew fiercely against the old door, the squeal of its rusty hinges sounding ominous in the sudden silence. Luke leaned his forehead against the wooden slats of the stall, exhausted in ways he couldn't even begin to name. He'd forgotten caring could hurt so much. Why couldn't he ever remember that?

He heard the shifting of straw and the soft pad of

footsteps as Sarah came to stand behind him. Even without the sound he would have known she was there. He could smell her. He could feel her. He sensed her as if she were another piece of him, separate yet still a part of his whole.

"I'm sorry," she said quietly, carefully. "I wouldn't hurt you, not for the world. I love you."

Love? Luke swung around, surprised beyond words. She couldn't love him, not a no-account like him. But the undisguised joy in her eyes left no room for doubt.

"I've loved you for a long time," she confessed, "maybe since that first night when you punched out Godzilla. I was afraid to admit it because of my past with Paul. I'm not afraid now."

He reached out and stroked her soft cheek, feeling her tremble exquisitely under his touch. *Love*, he thought, gazing down at her face in wonder. He was still a footloose drifter, and she was still a lady who deserved better. The small word changed nothing between them. And yet it changed everything.

"You know," he said truthfully, "if I were a decent man, I'd try my damnedest to talk you out of this."

She smiled, a wicked gleam in her eyes. "But you're not a decent man, are you?"

His mouth curved up in an answering grin. "No, I guess not."

NINE

Light shattered the sky. Startled, Sarah glanced at the open entrance to the barn; the door swung wildly on its hinges. "We ought to close—"

Luke pulled her roughly into his arms and shattered her with his own brand of lightning.

He consumed her lips, his practiced tongue savaging the sweet, vulnerable folds of her mouth. He tasted her deeply, devouring her with a primitive hunger that sent fire coursing through her body. A blast of thunder rattled the wooden walls, but she barely heard it. She was too mesmerized by the feel of him, the ravaging glory of his kiss, the seductive power of his hands as they smoothed down her sides and rubbed the sensitive crescent of her breasts. She pressed against him, feeling his heat sear her through the scant barrier of their wet clothing. Luke's carnal groan made her ache with wanton pleasure.

Yet it wasn't mere pleasure she wanted. She was driven by the primal need to give herself to this man, to let him find release and comfort in her body. She burned with that need, feeling it pound through her blood with every beat of her heart. Using instincts she didn't know she possessed, she ripped open the snaps of his shirt and buried her fingers in the soft, damp pelt covering his chest.

Luke pulled away and gazed down at her, the expression in his hooded eyes unreadable. Sarah froze in embarrassment. She'd wanted to show Luke how much she loved him and wanted him, but she should have waited for him to take the lead. Paul had been totally turned off the few times she'd taken the initiative. One time he'd even laughed at her efforts . . . a blush of shame heated her cheeks. "I'm sorry. I'm not very experienced at this—"

Luke pulled her to him in a crushing embrace, kissing her until she fell against his bare chest, shaking and breathless. Fighting for breath himself, he dropped down into the straw at the end of the stall and cradled her in his arms. "Darlin'," he said raspily, his voice carrying an unmistakable hint of humor, "if you get any more experienced, I'm a dead man."

"Really?" she said, blushing anew at his praise.

He smiled and tenderly brushed a strand of chestnut hair from her forehead. "You're the lawyer. Examine the evidence."

He circled her waist and moved her hips to straddle him, letting her softness discover his hard erection.

He rubbed against her, while erotically stroking her through the denim barrier of their jeans. Desire ripped through her, and she pressed closer, wild for the feel of him. Another carnal groan broke the silence, but this time it came from her throat.

He shucked off his shirt and helped her pull her own over her head. Sucking in his breath, he stared at her. His gaze caressed her breasts as intimately as his touch had. His undisguised passion gave her new confidence. She reached up and unclasped her bra, revealing herself completely to him. She knew she pleased him, but she wasn't prepared for what happened next.

He pulled her down on the straw with him. His callused thumb brushed fire across the tender nub of her breast. It was exquisite torture and she moaned with pleasure.

"You like this?" he asked, his leather-soft voice stroking her with its own caress.

She nodded, not trusting herself to speak. There had been lightning in his kiss; now lightning radiated from his touch, pooling into a sweet, savage inferno in her center. Every part of her shimmered with life. It was as if she'd been dead before—not just since her divorce, but every day of her existence. Until Luke came, she'd never known what living meant. Until he'd kissed her, she'd never known what it meant to be truly and richly alive.

Suddenly, his hands stilled. She moaned in protest, but he just grinned up at her, looking more like a

Cheshire cat than a hard-bitten cowboy. He's up to something, she thought. "Luke?"

Still grinning, he lifted her over him and took her breast into his mouth. She gasped as he sucked, his teeth and tongue executing the same shameless magic he'd performed on her mouth. She shuddered, barely able to breathe with wanting him. When he ended his caress, she collapsed on his chest, gasping for air. "Damn. Maybe I should have taken my chances on the roof."

He laughed, a deep, burnished sound that gave her more pleasure than she'd thought imaginable. She wanted to make him laugh again, every hour, every minute, until all the pain and hardships he'd suffered were erased from his memory. She grasped his shoulders and pulled herself over him, until she was nose-to-nose with his devilishly smiling face. "Okay, cowboy," she whispered, her tone ripe with mischievous challenge. "Now it's *my* turn."

She clasped her arms around his neck and kissed him with all the buried passion in her soul. Luke's surprise quickly turned to pleasure. He met her challenge with one of his own. Cries of passion intermingled with breathless laughter as they rolled together, each trying to outdo the other in the seduction game. Luke had experience on his side, but Sarah matched him point for point with originality and improvisation. By the time the straw stopped flying, they were both naked, and Luke lay on top of her, pinning her down with his body.

"Game's over," he growled, his breathing quick and shallow. "I win."

She nodded, laughing.

The smile on his face died, and his searching gaze locked on hers. "It's still your choice, Sarah."

She knew what he was asking. He didn't want only an afternoon of sex with her, or even a series of afternoons. He wanted something deeper, truer, and infinitely more personal. The need in his eyes reached right down through her to the bottom of her soul, and the intensity frightened her. She wasn't sure she was prepared for this kind of giving, but she knew that for his sake, she had to try.

She nodded again, never taking her gaze from his passion-dark eyes. "I know," she told him, and added in a husky whisper, "I love you."

He kissed her, robbing her of most of her breath and all of her senses. She arched to meet him, only to have him unexpectedly draw away. The sudden loss of his masculine weight and warmth reminded her how cold the cavernous barn was, and how empty. "Luke? What's wrong?"

"Nothing, darlin'," he said, covering her once again with his body. His fist opened, dropping a torn foil packet to the ground. "I just wanted to protect you."

She looked at the discarded packet, comprehension dawning. She was caught between appreciation for his thoughtfulness and resentment for his apparent experience with such matters. "Do you always carry one of those around?"

His deep chuckle caught her off-guard. "Why, Miss Sarah, I do believe you're jealous."

"Damn straight," she said, meeting his gaze.

"Well, don't be," he said quietly. "I started carrying one the first night I came here, and I've been going damn near crazy from not using it."

"The first night?" she murmured. "But I thought you couldn't stand me."

"I couldn't stand what you did to me." He raised himself over her so that she had no choice but to look directly into his fierce, burning eyes. "I've got no self-control when you're around. It's been that way from the start, ever since you walked into that seedy bar. On the ride out here a part of me wanted to haul you out to my truck and make love to you on the spot."

"I think part of me wanted you to," she confessed softly. "We've wasted so much time."

"We're here now," he said, placing his hot lips against the pulse point of her throat. "Give yourself to me now, Sarah. We'll make up for lost time. . . ."

Still caressing her neck, he reached down and stroked the soft thatch at the apex of her thighs. She opened to him with the grace of a flower, letting him test her readiness for him. She felt his fingers enter her moist heat and gasped as he caressed the swollen, aching lips of her sex. Her body exploded from the inside out. "Dammit, cowboy, you're driving me crazy."

"Then we're even," he growled, positioning himself over her.

He entered her slowly and smoothly, giving her

time to accept his full length. Still, he was more than she'd expected, possessing her more deeply than any man had before. Clinging to the strong columns of his shoulders, she felt a shudder pass through him and thought what a miracle it was that a world-weary man could take his ease in her body. She raised her hips, wanting to make his entry easier.

That movement was the last restraint either of them managed.

Suddenly, they were in the midst of a storm, as uncontrollable and wild as the one raging outside. He thrust into her, his body sending sheets of white-hot energy pouring through her. She bucked and writhed under him, consumed by the savage frenzy of their lovemaking. Lightning knifed through her, and her heart beat like thunder. The only thing keeping her from breaking apart was the burning intensity of Luke's hellfire eyes.

They moved together, two bodies and one heart, joined in the fire of their love. She clung to his sweat-sleek body, loving and fearing what he was doing to her. He pushed her to the edge, toppling her into a white-hot oblivion where nothing existed but her love for him. Then, after he'd watched the final passion blossom in her eyes, he shattered her again with the fury of his own release.

The storm had ended. Leftover raindrops dripped from the top beam of the barn's doorframe, falling into small puddles on the ground. A soft breeze blew through the opening, clean and rich with the promise of budding new life, and Sarah could see a silver of blue sky, and the mottled gold of sunlight as it burned away the dark anger of the clouds. Light and order returned to the world, but as she nestled closer to Luke's warm chest, she couldn't help feeling a little disappointed.

"The rain's stopped," she said, her voice tinged with regret.

Luke didn't answer. He lay back against the straw, one arm propped behind his head, the other holding her against him. His eyes were closed, and a smile graced his lips. He might have been asleep, except for the way his hand absently, erotically massaged her backside.

Sarah sighed, her breath a warm whisper against his chest. Happiness bloomed inside her. She felt as if all her life she'd been only half of a person, until Luke's love had made her whole. She'd never felt so contented, so fulfilled—or so hungry, she thought, glancing down at the strong, powerful lines of his naked form.

Sarah, you're turning into a sex maniac, she chided herself. Her practical nature reminded her of the chicken coop, the unmade dinner, and the numerous other chores that had to be done. Sighing again, this time with reluctance, she began to pull herself out of Luke's embrace.

His eyes still closed, his arm tightened around her

like a steel band. "And where do you think you're going?" he rumbled.

His rough voice spilled through her like sweet, hot honey. "Luke," she said, trying to fight her emotions, "we have to get back to work. Besides," she added, her gaze straying to the open barn door, "the children will be home in an hour."

He opened one eye. "A lot can happen in an hour," he said, grinning rakishly.

Sarah felt a hot blush creep up her neck. The man was incorrigible! "Don't be silly. I know the biological limits of the male, uh, physic. You can't possibly be ready to make love again."

Still smiling, he grasped her hips and moved her slightly over him, just enough to prove to her that he was not only ready but very able. Sarah's blush deepened.

"Do you know," he said tenderly, "that when you get embarrassed, you blush all over?" He lifted his hand and brushed his coarse knuckles across her sensitive nipples. "Even here."

She wasn't prepared for the shock of pure fire that shot through her at his gentle, teasing touch. "You're not making this easy," she accused.

He moved his hand and began to caress her breast. "I think I'm making it *real* easy."

"That's not . . ." Her words died as a stab of ecstacy rocked her. She ached for him, to have him caress her inside as thoroughly as he caressed her outside, yet part of her wanted to deny that need. She closed her eyes, shutting out the intimate fire in his intense blue gaze. "Luke, we can't do this. We have to get back to—"

"What are you afraid of?"

Her eyes flew open. She started to say she wasn't afraid but couldn't get the words out. Shaken, she realized Luke had uncovered a truth about herself she'd never faced before. "I'm not afraid, exactly," she confessed. "It's just that I'm not comfortable with making love in the daylight."

He arched an eyebrow. "You seemed pretty damned comfortable a little while ago."

"That was different. We were carried away by the moment. Now it would be . . . deliberate. You'd be watching me, measuring me against your other lovers." She shook her head, uncertain of how to explain her insecurity. "I mean, Paul used to say—"

One second Luke was lying relaxed on the straw pile beneath her; the next he was on top of her, effortlessly pinning her under him. "Don't ever mention that sorry fool to me again," he said, his anger barely contained. "He had his chance with you and blew it. Now it's my turn."

His lips came down on hers in a hard, plundering kiss. He kissed her ruthlessly, stroking and sucking her softness until she could barely move. Still, a small part of her held back, afraid to trust his promises.

He must have sensed her reserve. He lifted his head and gazed down at her, his eyes filled with quiet desperation. "Dammit, Sarah, I know about pain. I wrote the book on it. If you don't put it behind you, it will eat you up inside, like cancer." With profound tenderness he smoothed back her sweat-dampened hair. "He's not worth it."

She gazed at the rugged contours of his face, softened now by concern for her. Behind his outlaw facade was a man of great kindness and understanding—the man she'd fallen in love with. Yet beneath the kindness she sensed the jagged edge of bitterness, the deep hurt she'd felt in him ever since that first day. Luke understood her pain because he carried so much of his own with him. She knew all too well who had caused his pain. She lifted her hands and gently cupped his beard-roughened cheek as she quietly asked, "Is Annie worth it?"

He drew back as if she'd knifed him, then rolled off her and moved to the open end of the stall, crouching with his back to her. For a horrible moment she thought she'd pushed him too far and that he was going to leave, putting a wall between them that even her love couldn't breach. But he stayed where he was, as still as if he were carved in stone.

"It's was, not is," he said harshly. "Annie's dead."

His pain cut through to her own heart. "Oh, Luke, I'm so sorry," she said, moving to sit behind him. The muscles in his back were pulled taut as drawn wire. She reached out her hand to comfort him but pulled back at the last minute. Instinctively, she sensed that healing had to come from within himself. "Was she the person you lost in the accident?"

He nodded. "She was the best and brightest thing in my life." His words were soft as a prayer.

Sarah hated herself for the stab of jealousy she felt. She didn't want another woman, dead or living, sharing the heart of the man she loved. It was hard, very hard, to ignore the base emotion, but she did it for Luke's sake. She swallowed her pride. "Would you like to talk about her?"

"No," he stated. Then he looked at her over his shoulder, a curious smile on his lips. "But thanks. No one's ever offered to listen before."

Unexpectedly, her throat tightened, and her eyes brimmed with tears. She started to brush them away, but Luke turned around and reached out to do it for her.

"Why are you crying?"

"I don't know," she confessed. Love and sorrow and longing boiled inside her. She hated Annie, yet because Luke had loved her, Sarah loved her and mourned her death too. None of her emotions made sense, but they were the truest ones she'd ever felt. "I'm just so . . . sorry."

Luke's callused thumb stroked her cheek, gently wiping away her tears. "I guess we've both had our share of hard luck, haven't we?"

"I guess so," she agreed, her gaze fixed on his fathomless blue eyes. "I don't want to talk anymore, all right?"

He arched an eyebrow. "What do you want to do, Miss Sarah?"

She thought a moment. "I'd like to kiss you."

Luke's mouth twitched. "I'd like that too," he said, bending closer.

Sarah bit her lip, her eyes straying to another part of his anatomy. "Um, I didn't mean your mouth."

It took him a second to grasp her meaning. When he did, he threw back his head and let out a shout of laughter. "If I live to be a hundred, I'll never figure you out. What about you not wanting to make love in the daylight?"

"A woman can change her mind," Sarah said, smiling slowly. "Besides, if you can face your fears, I can certainly try to face mine."

"Crazy female," he murmured, his voice warm and potent as strong wine. He ran his eyes over her, his gaze touching her as intimately as a caress. Then, without warning, he stood up and swept her into his arms. "If we're going to make love *deliberately*, we're going to do it right," he said, carrying her toward the tack room. "I've got some protection in my room. Considering what's about to take place, I think we'd better use it."

Sarah clasped her arms around his neck and tried her best to look indignant. "You don't have to carry me."

He shook his head. "If I put you down, there's no telling where you'll run off to. I've never known a woman who can get into trouble quicker than you."

"I'm not that bad. Besides, I think you sort of enjoy rescuing me."

"Maybe," he admitted, as he set his shoulder against the door and effortlessly pushed it open, "but we're on a tight schedule here. There's some real important kissing to be done, and we've got less than an hour. . . ."

TEN

Life, Luke thought, as he sipped his second cup of coffee, was a lot like a woman. Just when you were certain it held no more surprises, and that you had every angle figured out from sideways to Sunday, it threw you a curveball. Grinning, he watched his particular curveball orchestrate the daily chaos of getting breakfast down her five little hell-raisers. Sarah's thick hair was rapidly escaping from her barrette, and a dab of grape jelly decorated her cheek. Still, he wouldn't have traded one glimpse of her for a runway full of fashion models. She was real and true and as honest as the sun that streamed in the kitchen window, lacing red fire through her unruly chestnut curls. And whenever she shot a shy look in his direction, he thought his heart would burst.

Barely a week had passed since that stormy afternoon in the barn, but Luke felt as if he'd lived a lifetime. Every moment he spent with Sarah shone with a new and precious joy. He'd never known that caring for someone could be so all-encompassing, that it could be an integral part of every hour of the day—and the night. His body tightened as he remembered the sweet, red-hot passion they'd shared not two hours before, when he'd woken up tangled in her hair and her body. Good thing he had some heavy work to do this morning. Otherwise, she might not make it out of the kitchen.

"Luke, what are you smiling at?" Micah asked.

I wish I had a nickel for every time this kid asked a question. "I was thinking about your mother," Luke said, keeping the answer as honest as decency allowed. "You know, if she ever gets tired of farming, there's an oil rig in the Gulf that would love to have her as a cook."

Sarah glanced at him over her shoulder, smiling wryly. "Oh, wow, my dream job. Cooking for forty."

"More like sixty," Luke confessed, taking a slow, deliberate sip of his coffee.

Her eyes followed the movement of his lips. Even across the width of the kitchen he heard the catch in her breathing and saw a rosy blush color her cheeks. He knew she was remembering another slow, deliberate act his lips had performed the night before.

The blare of the school-bus horn ended his imaginings. He pressed back against the counter, giving extra room to the five small cyclones who were leaving the kitchen. Plates chinked together, feet stomped, homework fluttered, and lunch bags crinkled as the kids stampeded for the back door. They yelled good-bye. He gave a brief salute in response. They were as loud and boisterous as a pack of wolf cubs, but Luke had to own he was getting sort of used to them.

He felt a slight tug on the leg of his jeans. Looking down, he saw Valerie standing beside him. "What's up, little bit?" he asked, hunkering down to her level.

She didn't answer. Instead, she threw her small arms around his neck and gave him a quick, impulsive kiss. Then she followed her siblings out the back door before he could say a word.

She needn't have hurried. Luke was in no condition to speak or even move. Val's feathery kiss had shaken him to his core. Old feelings surfaced, memories he'd buried so deep, he'd almost forgotten they existed. Suddenly unleashed, they roamed his soul like ancient, avenging monsters, tearing apart the fragile contentment in his heart.

The sleeping dragons . . .

"Luke?"

He raised his head. Through a haze of pain, he noted Sarah's concerned gaze. A few minutes ago her eyes had stirred profound love in his heart. Now he felt he faced a stranger.

"Luke, you don't have to feel embarrassed because Valerie kissed you."

Embarrassed? Sweet Jesus, if that's all it was! He rose and reached for his Stetson. "I'd best get started on the repairs."

Sarah's expressive eyes widened into genuine alarm. "What's wrong? You're acting so strangely."

"How I act is my business, not yours," he said curtly.

A look of pain crossed her face. Damn, he'd never meant to hurt her, but he couldn't handle her questions. Sarah was as much a part of him as his bones and blood. If she probed too deeply, she'd know. He settled his hat on his head, pulling down the brim to shield his eyes from her searching gaze. "Got to see to the—"

"Dammit, Luke, you can't leave it like this!" Sarah cried, blocking his path to the door. "I love you. Don't shut me out. Please, talk to me."

He wanted to. God, how he wanted to! He ached to tell her everything, to unburden his soul like a sinner to a father confessor. But Sarah was no priest. And there were some sins that could never be forgiven. "You don't know what you're asking."

"Then tell me," she pleaded as she reached up and gently cupped his jaw. "I'm not a mind reader. If you don't talk to me, I can't help you."

"I don't want your help," he snarled, roughly shaking off her touch. "I want you to leave me alone!"

"Fine!" she fired back, bright temper masking the pain of betrayal. "I won't bother you anymore. You can go straight to hell, for all I care."

For a long moment their gazes locked, joined in a battle too deep for words. Luke stared into her green eyes, seeing every emotion in her honest, valiant soul shining in their radiant depths. He'd never loved her more than at that moment, but he kept his feelings hidden behind the cold, stony glare of his own eyes. She deserved a decent man's full heart, not the broken, battered ruin of emotion that he had to offer. He loved her too much to let her settle for less than she deserved.

He stalked away, determined to leave before he lost his resolve. He yanked open the screen door but paused for a second in the doorway. "Don't try to dig too deep," he warned in a voice as rough and dusty as gravel. "You may not like what you find."

"He's a jerk," Sarah muttered as she rigorously scrubbed the bathtub tile. "He's arrogant, and selfish, and egotistical, and—"

And she was falling more in love with him every day.

She threw down her cloth, uttering a curse that would have caused Jenny to blush. It made her feel better, but not much. She sat on the edge of the tub, lacing her fingers in tight frustration. Damn the man! She'd told him about her past. It was only fair that he tell her about his.

Fair is where you take your—

"Don't say it!" she cried aloud, censuring the ghostly memory of her great-aunt's advice. "It isn't fair. Luke ought to tell me about his past. Why won't he?"

Silence was her only reply.

Grumbling anew, she cast her gaze around her bathroom, looking for something else to scrub. During her courtroom days she'd discovered that the best way to work through her problems was to clean something—the nastier, the better. Focusing on something mindless helped jog her creative powers to come up with new ideas and solutions. But the only thing she'd jogged so far was her thumb on the toilet rim. She hadn't made any progress in her dilemma with Luke, even though her bathroom gleamed.

Unbidden, her thoughts drifted back to the day when Luke had rescued Benny the brontosaurus from her sink. The sudden sexual heat that had flared between them had turned the little room into an inferno. But it wasn't his body that had seduced her. It was his vulnerability—the rough gentleness of his big hands when he'd wiped Valerie's toy, his endearing bewilderment at her numerous bottles and jars, the passionate longing in his eyes when he'd asked her not to answer the doorbell. She had been falling in love with him for weeks, but that afternoon was the first time she'd realized how much he needed her.

For now, anyway . . .

Dammit, she'd been so careful not to think about the future! She and Luke never talked about it when they were together. She told herself this was because the feelings between them were too new, too unsettled, but in her heart of hearts she knew there probably wasn't going to be a future for her and Luke.

He was a drifter, free as the wind, while she was tied to a run-down farm and five rambunctious children. She'd known the truth from the start. She had gone into their relationship with her eyes wide open. She just hadn't expected to love him quite so much.

This wasn't getting her anywhere! She left the bathroom and its memories behind, striding through her room until she reached the hall. But her doubts followed her, nipping at her heels like hounds on the scent of a fox. She leaned her forehead against a nearby doorframe, groaning miserably.

The door led to Valerie's room. Glancing inside, she caught sight of Mr. Bear sitting regally on the pink comforter. His shiny black eyes seemed to stare right at her. He looked so wise, so understanding. . . .

Hell, she'd had conversations with roosters and the memory of her dead great-aunt. Why not have one with a stuffed animal? She walked into the room and sat down on the pink comforter, smoothing the satin material with her palm.

"Luke's a proud, pigheaded man," she stated.

Mr. Bear gave her no argument on that score.

"Of course," she added, "to be fair, he's also a decent man. And honest. And one of the gentlest men I've—" She felt the sudden sting of tears in her eyes. "Dammit, why did I have to fall in love with him?"

Mr. Bear definitely had no answers for that one.

Sighing, Sarah drew up her legs and wrapped her arms around them, laying her cheek against her knees.

"I won't have him forever, I know that. But before he goes, I wish I could do something to ease the hurt inside him. It's eating him alive, Mr. Bear. Bit by bit.

"He warned me not to dig too deep. He's afraid I'll be disappointed in him, maybe even stop loving him—as if I ever could." Her lips curved into a bittersweet smile as she remembered how Luke had sat on this bed and sung Valerie to sleep with the *Flintstones'* theme. "I don't know what kind of man he was, but I know what kind of man he is. I can see the goodness in him. Why can't he?"

Mr. Bear didn't have to reply to that one either. She already knew the answer. As a public defender she'd seen how a troubled past could warp a person. She'd seen ordinary, innocent people beaten and broken by the arbitrary disasters fate had thrown their way. All too often they bottled up their rage until it ate away all their faith and hope. She'd learned that adversity didn't build character—it destroyed it. She'd learned that real happiness was an elusive commodity, rarer and more precious than diamonds.

But she had that elusive happiness when she was with Luke, and she believed he had it when he was with her. "He may not trust me with his past," she told her stuffed companion, "but he's trusted me with his present. And while he's here, I'm going to love him just as much and hard as I can, even if he does make me mad as hell sometimes."

She slipped off the bed, feeling more refreshed

than she had all morning. She paused at the door and gave Mr. Bear a parting smile. "If I'd known you were such a good listener, I would have gladly bypassed cleaning the bathroom."

It was probably a trick of the light, but she could have sworn that Mr. Bear winked at her.

He knew she was behind him. The strange awareness they shared alerted him to her approach. His heart jumped with a crazy, pointless hope that he wasn't quite able to kill. He shifted the hose he was using to fill the water trough to his other hand. *Keep this up, and you'll have to turn this hose on yourself.*

"Er, hot, isn't it?" Sarah said.

She doesn't know the half of it. Earlier he'd taken off his shirt and gloves to combat the burning heat of the midday sun. But there was no easy cure for the heat that built inside him whenever she was near. With his free hand he pulled his hat off and used his forearm to mop the sweat from his brow. "You came all the way out here to tell me that?"

"No. I came out here because I want to be with you."

Damn the woman! Couldn't she even stay angry with him properly? He twisted around to look at her, determined to give her the iciest stare and the sharpest put-down in his personal arsenal. But the sight of Sarah's bright eyes, her wind-mussed hair, and her shy, uncertain smile gutted his ferocity. He turned his back to her. "Go back to the house, Sarah," he warned gruffly.

She didn't reply. Instead, she walked around him, apparently taking great interest in the trough he was filling. "This was full yesterday, wasn't it?"

Luke didn't want to talk about the trough, or anything else, for that matter. Having her within arm's length was shifting his hormones into overdrive. For the last week he'd had free rein to satisfy the physical and emotional madness that quickened inside him whenever she was near. Now he had to pull himself back from that freedom, and his body liked it about as much as a green colt liked its first taste of the saddle.

Anger hadn't worked. Retreat was his next-best option. He reached down and cut off the water, then looped the length of hose over the peg near the spigot. "Someone punched a hole in the trough last night," he said without thinking, eager to put distance between himself and her sweet, vulnerable smile. "Now I'll see to those fences in the far—"

"What do you mean, 'Someone punched a hole in it'?"

Uh-oh. Too late he remembered that he hadn't told her about the minor incidents of vandalism that had been occurring on the farm. Now did not seem the ideal time to break the news. "Did I say 'someone'? I meant 'something.' "

"Something like an ice pick," Sarah commented. She bent down and examined his repair job, then glanced up at Luke with wary, perceptive eyes. "I haven't seen this sort of thing since I left Dallas. What's going on, Luke?"

He sighed, wishing he could spare her but knowing she'd get the truth out of him sooner or later. "Someone's been causing some damage around the farm. It's only pranks, really. Kid stuff, nothing serious."

"Nothing serious?" she cried, rising to face him. "Someone's been vandalizing my farm! You should have told me. We've got to call the authorities."

"Oh, right," Luke drawled, "I'm sure the sheriff's gonna rush right over here to investigate a bunch of schoolboy pranks, especially since you're such a valued member of this community."

She couldn't help but catch the sarcasm in his tone and lifted her chin defiantly. "The law is the law."

"Correction, Brennermen is the law, at least in this county," he stated with unvarnished honesty. "He practically had Jenny charged with a crime she didn't commit. What makes you think he won't try to pin this vandalism on one of your kids?"

"But he can't, he wouldn't. . . ." Her words faded as swiftly as her confidence. She grew still, and her eyes took on the haunted expression he hadn't seen in them for weeks. She wrapped her arms around herself, looking fragile and frightened and heartbreakingly alone. "Someone's been on my land. It's a horrible feeling, even if they didn't do much harm. I really wish you'd told me."

So did Luke. He'd kept silent because he'd wanted to protect her but had ended up hurting her even more. It killed him to see her like this, to watch her valiant spirit brought low by fear. He wanted like hell to wrap her in his arms and promise her everything would be all right, but he doubted she'd believe him. He doubted she'd ever believe him again. He'd betrayed her with his silence. Her softly voiced words rang with it.

He pulled off his hat and fingered the brim, wishing hearts were as easy to mend as water troughs. "Well," he said quietly, "maybe the next guy you fall in love with will have more sense than I do."

Her head whipped up. "The next guy?" she repeated, staring at him with wide, furious eyes.

"Sarah, don't get riled—"

His words fell on deaf ears. "How dare you?" she said, seething. "Do you think I fall in love with every man who crosses my path?"

"No, I—"

"Damn straight I don't!" She planted her fists on her waist and glared at him with barely contained rage. "Honestly, cowboy, sometimes you make me so mad I could—"

He caught the glimmer of intent in her eyes, but by then it was too late. Quicker than lightning she reached out and snatched his Stetson, then dangled it menacingly over the water trough.

"Hey, give that back!"

"I will not," she said without a trace of remorse.

"It'd serve you right if I dunked this hat. In fact, I think I will."

Luke could understand that she was upset. But threatening a man's hat—that was going too far. He lunged at her and caught her arms, determined to wrestle his Stetson from her grasp. Unfortunately, she was ready for him. She deftly hooked her leg around the back of his knee, pulling him off-balance. Cursing, Luke threw his weight to the side to avoid crushing her in a fall and ended up toppling them both into the water trough. His hat, ironically, fell to the ground unharmed.

The water wasn't deep—when he sat up, it barely reached his breastbone. Still, he'd landed facedown in the trough and ended up thoroughly drenched. "Damn, woman," he sputtered as he coughed out a mouthful of water, "what *is* it with you and getting wet?"

Sarah laughed, a bright, unexpected sound that danced along his nerve endings like pure electricity. The woman had no sense of propriety. Worse yet, her laughter was contagious. He found himself laughing right along with her.

As her laughter dwindled, she lifted her arm to push back her heavy hair, unconsciously emphasizing the swell of her breasts against her wet T-shirt. Soaked to the skin, her lush body looked like every teenage boy's fantasy—and Luke felt all of sixteen. A raw fire totally at odds with his sodden state began to build in his belly.

"Sarah," he said thickly, "I think we'd better—"

He got no further. In the space of a heartbeat Sarah was pressed against him, clinging to him like a second skin. Water droplets hung off her thick, feathery lashes, and her impossibly expressive eyes shone with anguish. She trembled in his arms. "Please, don't push me away."

"I've got to," he said miserably, though he couldn't quite make his arms obey his command. "I always hurt people I care about. I'm no good, Sarah. You don't know what I've done—"

"I don't care." She dipped her head to his neck and brushed warm, wet kisses across his collarbone. "The past and future don't matter," she murmured. "All that matters is now. I love you, Luke. Let me love you."

He held firm to his resolve—for about five seconds. Then the sheer power of his need for her demolished his good intentions. Lust he could handle, but what he felt for Sarah went way beyond physical desire. Groaning, he twisted his fingers in her hair and brought her lips to his in a ruthless kiss.

She tasted like sunshine and laughter, and all the sweet pleasures his used-up soul desperately needed. He plundered her softness with his teeth and tongue until she fell, spent and shivering, against him. Then he lowered his head for more.

Kisses weren't enough. He pushed up her shirt and pulled aside her bra, tearing the lace in his urgency. He filled his hand with her sensitive, swelling breast, needing to brand her with his hot touch and claim her.

She arched against him, pressing herself deeper into his caressing hand, telling him without words that she loved his rough seduction. She trailed soft, desperate kisses across his chest and the bunched muscles of his upper arms, branding him with a sweet fire all her own. Wordlessly, frantically, they moved against each other, churning the trough water.

Time was his enemy. She'd said now was all they had, but he knew in his heart that a hundred thousand nows would never give him enough of her. He ran his palms down the smooth skin of her sides and back, loving her tiny whimpers of pleasure against his chest and throat. He dipped his hands below the waterline, growling with appreciation as she shucked her cutoffs to be naked from the waist down.

He took her lips again, possessing her mouth as his hands possessed her thighs and bottom. No woman had ever tasted so sweet or craved his touch with such ardent pleasure. He devoured her like a condemned man's last meal, feasting on her passion, her joy, her love. Red madness rose in him, almost overwhelming his conscience. Almost.

He felt her work his belt free and pull his jeans to his knees. He breathed a raw curse of both pleasure and pain, belatedly realizing he wasn't prepared for this. Struggling with himself as much as her, he trapped her clever hands and held her still. "Sarah, stop."

She didn't. Instead, she moved against him, showing him that trapping only her hands wasn't going to do him a bit of good.

"Sarah, for the love of God." He groaned. "I haven't got a condom!"

Her wide, loving eyes seemed to burn clear through to his thundering heart. "Then take me without one," she whispered. "Just once, take everything I have to offer."

After that, nothing in heaven or earth could have stopped him. He took her hips and lifted her over his arousal, sinking into her velvet heat in one shattering thrust. She caressed him inwardly, her body instinctively giving him the same loving touch as her lips and her hands. Wondrously, he realized that her love for him was deep and abiding, despite the hurts he'd caused her, despite her uncertainty about his past. She loved him with the simplicity of the sunshine, the bright, blazing sunshine that poured life and light into his barren soul. He moved within her, taking and giving back the life she offered in a blinding release, until they burned together in the heart of a new sun.

Afterward he cradled her against him, gentling her as she came back from the ravaging joy of their lovemaking. He took a deep breath of the spring breeze, wondering when the air had grown so sweet and when the sky had gotten so blue. He searched his soul for the anger and bitterness that had always been so much a part of him, but the sleeping dragons were gone.

There was no room in his heart for anything but Sarah.

He smoothed her hair, carefully shifting her body until his lips were next to her ear. Then he whispered the words he'd never spoken to a living soul since Annie's death.

"I love you."

ELEVEN

"Rats." Micah stood in the middle of the dining room, stretching a crepe-paper streamer. "It's too short to reach the wall. What do I do now?"

"Tape it to the ceiling," Jenny suggested. She was attaching a paper sunflower to the chandelier and looked over at Micah through the crystal prisms. "I told Rafe we should have bought more."

"Well, we could have if you hadn't made me get those stupid paper flowers," Rafe answered. He and Lyn with questionable assistance from Valerie and Mr. Bear were lettering a sign.

Jenny bristled. "They're not stupid flowers. They're pretty."

"They're dumb, Spots."

"Are not!"

"Are too!"

"Kids!" Sarah cried as she hurried in from the

kitchen, baster still in hand. "We don't have time for fighting. Luke will be here any minute, and you're not even half done with the decorations. I need you to work together—quietly. Think you can do that?"

"Okay," Rafe grumbled.

"Sure." Jenny shot Rafe a withering glare. "But only for Luke."

For Luke. The words echoed hollowly in Sarah's mind as she returned to the kitchen and her half-basted turkey. The children had organized this surprise party for Luke entirely on their own, a feat of diplomacy that the United Nations would have been hard-pressed to match. They wanted to show him how much they appreciated all the hard work he'd done to get the farm in shape for tomorrow's inspection—the inspection that marked the end of Luke's employment at Corners.

Sarah shoved the turkey back in the oven and shut the door with a bang. She stood up, smoothing the dark, ankle-length broomstick-pleated skirt she'd donned for the party, along with a white peasant blouse embroidered with emerald green that matched her eyes. She'd braided her heavy hair back in an unusually neat French braid that hung down almost to her waist. She'd primped for an hour over her appearance, feeling as giddy as a teenager preparing to go on her first big date. But as the time of the party drew closer, she felt less and less like celebrating.

She sighed and lifted the lid on the green beans almandine, giving the mixture an unnecessary stir.

She considered making yet another kind of vegetable for variety, but she'd already cooked up five separate dishes and doubted she could find room on the counter. She'd baked all afternoon, producing enough food to feed her family five times over. It kept her mind off Luke—sort of. And it was a damn sight better than cleaning her spotless bathroom again.

So what's the big surprise, counselor? You've always known he'd be moving on after the inspection.

Yes, she'd known—but it hurt so much.

She heard a commotion in the dining room. Lord, her kids were at it again! Sighing, she headed for the door and pushed it open, ready once more to try to put an end to Rafe and Jenny's bickering.

They weren't fighting. Luke had arrived, and the children were gathered around him, vying loudly for his attention. He wore a soft cotton shirt the color of buckskin and his best pair of jeans, looking every inch the honored guest. Sarah smiled, recalling that he'd found out about the kids' party days ago but had decided to let them "surprise" him anyway.

She wondered if Luke regretted his decision. He had just enough time to set his beloved old Stetson on the sideboard, safely out of harm's way, before the kids literally dragged him over to see their newly—and crookedly—hung banner.

"We only had time to put one *L* in your last name," Rafe explained. "Lyn wrote the 'Congratulations on Your New Job,' and I added the 'Good Luck.'"

Valerie pulled forcefully on his pant leg and pointed to a corner of the banner. "Me and Mr. Bear did the butterflies."

Val's drawings looked more like bugs than butterflies, but Luke didn't seem to mind. He bent down and scooped up the little girl, holding her easily in the crook of his arm. "They're real pretty butterflies. I can tell all of you worked hard on these decorations. Thanks."

Thanks. That one simple word made her wary children light up like Roman candles. They'd put their hearts into planning Luke's party, hearts that had been trampled on by so many others. His sincere appreciation had done them more good than a year's worth of counseling. *He's made such a difference in all our lives*, Sarah thought, blinking back sudden tears. *Whatever happens, whatever the cost, I'm glad he came.*

She cleared her throat, determined not to let her bleak mood spoil the children's fun. "Glad you could make it, cowboy," she said brightly.

Luke turned around, Valerie still in his arms. His blue gaze drew her like the azure heart of a flame. The room faded around her, and for a moment it seemed that they were the only two people in the world. Then Valerie squirmed, breaking the spell.

"Luke's here, Sarah. Can we eat now?"

"Well, I see Val's got her priorities straight," Luke said, laughing, as he lowered the girl gently to the ground. "How about we get this thing started?"

The meal that followed was, by anyone's stand-ards, one to remember. Seating was the first catastro-phe. Each child wanted to sit by Luke. Sarah finally outyelled the lot of them, choosing Lyn and Micah because they were the quietest. The others sulked through grace, although their spirits brightened con-siderably when Luke started carving the turkey. Peace reigned for a whole five minutes—until Micah took it upon himself to explain the human digestive process, in graphic detail.

Things got progressively more hectic, defying even the household's usual standards for pandemonium. Valerie accidentally dripped cranberry sauce on Mr. Bear, and then cried because it looked like he was bleeding. Rafe and Jenny argued over everything from passing the salt to ownership of the last drumstick. Sarah gritted her teeth against a growing headache and prayed that God would help the rest of Luke's party to go smoothly. The words of the prayer still echoed in her mind when their rambunctious watchdog, Schwarzy, bounded into the dining room, dragging his broken leash behind him. He was snout-deep in the mashed potatoes before Luke and the boys wrestled him under control.

But the worst was yet to come. When Sarah and the children cleared away the dishes for pie and ice cream, Rafe scooted out into the hall and reappeared holding a large box. "We all chipped in to buy this," he explained as he handed the present to Luke. "We wanted to give you something to remember us by."

Instantly, Sarah forgot the previous chaos. She glanced around at her children, proud of them in a whole new way. Their gift was as much of a surprise to her as it was to Luke. Her kids had done this on their own, out of love for the drifter who had stumbled so inadvertently and completely into all of their hearts. The disasters of the evening counted for nothing. *Luke's part of our family,* she realized. *No matter where he goes, or who he's with, he'll always be part of our family.* The thought helped to ease the ache inside her. A little.

Sarah watched as Luke opened the gift, as eager as he was to see what was inside. The shape of the present looked vaguely familiar, though she couldn't exactly place it. The box was big, a little wider than a man's head, but she knew from the easy way Rafe had handled it that the contents weren't very heavy. She leaned closer, curious to know what special present her kids had chosen to give the man who had come to mean so much to them all. Big, light, wider than a man's head . . .

Sarah froze. They couldn't. They wouldn't.

They had.

Luke slowly lifted the new Stetson out of the box. It was a stunning piece of work, with a six-inch cattleman-creased crown and a leather band studded with fine concha silver. The felt was so shiny, it gleamed.

Luke held it as if he were holding a rattler.

Lyn came to his side. "We noticed your hat was

getting pretty old, so we thought you could use a new one. You like it, don't you?"

Like the plague, Sarah thought, feeling helpless. Her well-meaning kids had managed to give Luke the one present in the world he least wanted. She knew how much he treasured his battered old Stetson. The hat was a part of him, more like a trusted friend than a piece of clothing.

As if he read her thoughts, Luke glanced over at the sideboard and the worn Stetson that rested there, safely out of reach of children, dogs, and other predictable disasters. He gave the hat a long, wistful look, then set the stiff new Stetson firmly on his brow. "Thanks, kids. It's just what I needed."

And Sarah lost it. She'd held her emotions in check throughout the party, but the sight of Luke willingly giving up his cherished hat to please her children was too much for her to bear. She whirled abruptly and fled into the kitchen and out through the back door to the porch. She knew she'd made a spectacle of herself, but she didn't care. She felt as if she were about to explode.

A cool summer evening was settling over her world. Blue shadows lengthened across the yard, and the sweetly pungent smell of sage blossoms filled the air, but Sarah hardly noticed. She gripped the porch rail, shaking from the fury of the emotions within her. She felt all cut up inside, like a mirror that had been shattered into a million razor-sharp shards. The broken pieces still reflected her image, but it was a strange, misshapen creature. Without Luke's love she could barely recognize herself. Without Luke's love there seemed little point in trying.

She heard the screen door open and shut behind her. Heavy, measured steps walked up to the rail beside her. She didn't need to look to see who it was. Even his footsteps were dear to her.

"Are you all right?" Luke asked.

Sarah nodded, not daring to look at him. "I'm only thinking . . . about the inspection."

He leaned against the railing, the old wood protesting under his weight. "It's not like you to lie, Sarah," he said quietly.

She drew in a deep breath of the night and tried again. "They gave you a hat."

Luke's chuckle rumbled through the quiet air. "They surely did," he said, touching the brim of his new Stetson. "It'll take some getting used to."

Sarah shook her head, still staring out into the darkness. "But you *love* your old hat."

"Well, I'll learn to love this one." Then, in a tone as soft as the night around them, he added, "A man can change, Sarah."

A man can change. She looked up at him and saw the question in his eyes and the uncertainty in his cocksure smile. He wasn't talking about his hat. He was talking about something deeper, truer, and as impossible to explain as the glory of a star-filled sky. Yet she understood every unspoken word. She swallowed, choosing her words more carefully than she ever had. "It's a hat made to last," she said huskily. "One that will stick with you through thick and thin, no matter what happens."

"Till death do us part?" he whispered.

She lifted her hand to his Stetson and skimmed her fingers reverently along the finished edge. "Longer."

And then she was in his arms, his hellfire kiss branding his mark on her soul. She staked her own passionate claim, weaving her hands through his hair with such fury that it knocked the hat from his head. She didn't notice. She was too caught up in the joy of loving and being loved, and the knowledge that, whatever the future held, they would face it together.

Laughing, crying, she fell against him, her fingers bunching and rebunching the soft material of his shirt. Happiness made her weak. She raised her head and stared up at his hard, dear face, and saw his eyes soften with undisguised love. He reached up and gently tucked a strand of hair behind her ear, then followed his fingers with his lips. The teasingly erotic caress promised a lifetime of pleasure. She moaned, undone by his cherishing tenderness and the love that lay behind it. *He was going to stay; he was really going to stay. . . .*

"So," he murmured against her ear, "where's a man find a preacher in this county?"

"Preacher?" She was too caught up in the ecstacy of his touch to fully comprehend him.

"Yeah, a preacher. The nearest one." His warm

breath tickled her ear. "Right now I'm not too choosy about the denomination."

Understanding pricked her passion-fevered mind. She pushed away from his chest and looked up at him, a cold dread growing inside her. "Why do you want a preacher?"

"Why do you think I want a preacher?" he said, grinning broadly. "I haven't checked up on it lately, but last time I heard, you needed one of them to get properly spliced."

"You want to ... marry me?"

"Of course I do. That's what we've been talking about, isn't it?"

No, it wasn't. He'd simply told her he wasn't going to leave her. She wanted him to stay, more than anything. But marriage?

Memories of her disastrous marriage to Paul filled her mind. She'd spent years trying to win back the love of a man whose heart was committed to someone else. She knew Luke loved her—it wasn't a question of that—but he loved Annie more. Dead or living, she knew Luke's former lover would always hold the first place in his heart. Sarah would never be more than second-best.

It was enough, Sarah told herself. If secondhand love was the best he could give her, she'd take it and be grateful for it. But to stand up in a church, before God and everyone, and make him lie for her ... that she would not do.

"Can't we go on being lovers?"

Luke shook his head. "No, we can't. I'm tired of sneaking around, like our love was something to be ashamed of. I'm proud that I love you, and I want the world to know it. I want to tell the whole county— including Brennermen—that if he messes with you again, he'll have me to contend with. I want to give you my name and my protection, and to be a father to your kids, if they'll have me. I want you to be my wife, Sarah." He paused, and gave her a puzzled look. "I thought you'd want that too."

A sudden chill wind blew across the porch, making her shiver. "Luke, I love you with all my heart, but . . . I can't marry you."

If he'd yelled at her, if he'd called her names, even if he'd cursed her, she could have taken it. Instead, he stood there, saying nothing. His expression hardened, and his eyes took on a deadly sheen. When he finally did speak, his slow words carried a lethal bite. "I see."

Sarah didn't like the sound of that. "I don't think you do. I—"

"Spare me, Sarah." He stalked to the other side of the porch, cursing soundly. "I'm the hired help— good enough to sleep with but not good enough to marry. We've been through this before."

Luke's words hit her like a physical blow. She'd said she loved him and proved it in a hundred different ways. "You can't honestly believe that."

"You make it damn near impossible to believe anything else!" Still glowering, he walked back to her and scooped up the Stetson at her feet. "Well," he stated as he set it determinedly on his head, "at least I got a decent hat out of it."

Oh, sometimes he could be so infuriating! She glared at him, hands on her hips, her voice just as lethal as his. "Luke Tyrell, you are going to listen to me if I have to hog-tie you to the porch railing!"

She never got a chance to make good on her threat. At that moment a cry cut the night, high and wailing, the crow of a terrified rooster. "It's Cogburn," she said as she leaned over the railing and peered through the darkness toward the chicken coop. "But he's never crowed before."

Luke instantly appeared at her side. "Something's spooked him. Something . . . dear Lord!"

He vaulted over the railing and sprinted toward the barn. Sarah's long skirt made a similar maneuver impossible. She took the steps two at a time and raced after him. A stray breeze carried the smell of smoke to her nostrils. Instantly alert, she glanced toward the barn. Bright orange licked out from under its rafters.

Sweet Jesus, her barn was on fire!

TWELVE

He knew fire. He'd battled it many times over the years, everything from a small grease blaze in a drover's kitchen out West to a hellfire explosion on a Gulf oil rig that took several lives before it was put out. He'd learned to respect fire, never to take it for granted, and always to expect the unexpected. Most of all, he'd learned how to tell the difference between a fire that could be brought under control and one that would rage away until it eventually burned itself out.

Sarah's old barn hadn't a hope in Hades of surviving.

"Get back to the house and call for help," he shouted to Sarah. "The fire hasn't spread to the main part of the barn, but it's gotten into the rafters. I can't put it out on my own."

"You're not on your own, cowboy."

He looked at her. Red firelight cast living shadows on her face, making it impossible to read her expression. But the determined stance of her body, straight and fierce as a soldier facing battle, told him she had no intention of leaving him. She was the most obstinate, mule-stubborn woman he'd ever met, and he'd love her till the day he died, if he didn't strangle her first.

"Get back to the house," he ordered curtly. "Or I'll—"

He never finished his threat. Suddenly, he caught sight of two figures running out of the barn, two small shadows silhouetted against the light. Kids. "What the . . . ?"

"Jill! Becky!" Sarah cried, apparently recognizing the children. She ran to meet them and fell to her knees, hugging the frightened girls against her. "There, there. It's going to be all right."

All right? Luke thought as he glanced at the burning barn. All right was the one thing it was definitely *not* going to be. He recalled the recent vandalism, the pranks that had childish mischief stamped all over them. He'd bet his last dollar that the sobbing kids Sarah held in her arms were the mysterious tricksters, caught one prank too late.

Becky's tearful words confirmed his suspicions. "We didn't mean to. It was only supposed to be a little fire. Little like all the other things."

Jill nodded, sobbing in unison. "We didn't want to, but Cathy said—"

"Cathy Brennermen?" Luke asked harshly. "*She* put you up to this?"

"She said we wouldn't hurt anything, not really," Becky confided. "Didn't you, Cathy? Cathy?"

Both girls looked around, searching for their leader but not finding her. Luke turned to face the steadily growing blaze, the rising heat at odds with the sudden cold in the pit of his stomach. *Good Lord, the kid must still be inside.*

He was startled out of his thoughts by the gunshot slam of the screen door. Sarah's children tumbled out of the house, yelling with fright and excitement. Only Lyn showed presence of mind, promptly heading back inside, yelling that she was going to call for help. The rest of them started down the porch steps.

"Get back in the house!" Luke commanded, fear making his words overloud. The thought of the kids near the fire frightened him almost as much as having Sarah there. With a clarity born of a dire situation, he realized it wasn't only Sarah he'd fallen in love with, but her children as well.

His command stopped the kids in their tracks. Gratified that at least *some* of the people he loved could follow orders, he swung around and started toward the barn. He was quickly taking in details—matching the sight, the smell, and the taste of this fire against the ones he'd battled in the past. It was fierce, but it hadn't yet spread to the main area of the building. He could go in through the tack room. With a little luck—

His thoughts ended abruptly as awareness pricked his soul, an awareness that came only from the presence of one special woman. He didn't need to turn around to know she was following him. "Go back, Sarah," he said, keeping his gaze on the fire.

"No," she stated, falling into step beside him. "You might need my help."

Luke heard the determination in her voice and knew he had a better chance of changing the course of the Rio Grande than Sarah's mind. Lord, why couldn't he have fallen in love with a sensible woman? "What I need most," he said quietly, "is to know that you and the kids are safe."

He heard the catch in her breathing and stole a quick look at her beautiful, expressive eyes. Love shone in them, brighter and fiercer than any flame. But fear was there too. He opened his mouth, searching for words to comfort her, and found none.

He swung his gaze back to the barn and ran full out toward it, relieved that Sarah didn't follow. He had to keep focused if he was going to get the Brennermen girl out of that tinderbox. Already the flames were beginning to lick out of the far end of the barn. He had ten, maybe fifteen, minutes to get in, find Cathy, and get both of them out before the roof came down.

Time was precious, yet he paused at the tack-room door, unable to resist one last look at Sarah. She stood where he'd left her, hands on hips in her familiar soldier's stance, waiting. He knew with a certainty that she'd wait for him outside the gates of hell itself if that was what he wanted. Plain loco, that's what she was. And he loved every crazy inch of her.

Sarah saw him turn and raised her hand in a salute. "Be careful," she called.

"Count on it. You're not going to get out of marrying me that easy," he yelled back. Then he turned back and plunged without hesitation into the brimstone world of the growing inferno.

The sheriff's deputy lowered the microphone of his car radio and spoke to Sarah. "The paramedics will be here in a minute, ma'am."

"That's what you said a minute ago. And a minute before that," she said tersely. She stabbed her finger toward the steadily burning barn. "Two people are in there."

"I know, ma'am," the young officer replied, sounding genuinely frustrated. "But there's nothing we can do until the paramedics arrive. We don't have the equipment to go in—"

"Neither did Luke!" she cried. She cursed in anguish, her patience worn as thin as the edge of a knife. The fire was growing more fierce by the moment.

Tongues of red and orange licked the night sky, consuming the darkness even as it consumed the sturdy timber of her ancient barn. She brushed her sweat-damp hair off her forehead and found the back of her hand streaked with soot and ash. Lord, if it was this bad out in the open, what must it be like inside? It had been ten minutes since Luke had entered the barn—ten eternities. Time seemed to be moving like molasses.

She couldn't stand this waiting. All her life she'd been the kind of person who made things happen. She had taken the initiative and put her thoughts and beliefs into action, even when those actions were unpopular. As a defense attorney she'd invariably argued the lost causes. She'd adopted her problem children against the advice of her friends and family. She'd chosen to live at Corners despite community disdain. Sometimes her actions had solved her problems. Sometimes they'd created more, but she'd always been able to make a choice and act on it. Until now.

The wave of fear she'd been holding back threatened to overwhelm her. The man she loved was in danger, and there wasn't a thing she could do about it. She'd never felt so helpless.

The sudden roar of an approaching car interrupted her thoughts. Her heart leaped in the belief that the paramedics had arrived at last. But her hope died as she realized it was only an ordinary car, albeit one that was being driven at top speed. The black Chevy careened into her driveway, its spinning tires sending gravel flying. The driver got out, leaving the door open, and hurried toward the deputy's patrol car.

It was Brennermen.

"Where's my daughter?" he demanded in his bull-horn voice. "The sheriff said she was here."

The young deputy, apparently cowed by the presence of the most powerful man in the county, fished around ineffectually for a reply. "She's, uh. Well, she's—"

"She's in the barn," Sarah said. She harbored no love for Brennermen, but as Cathy's father, he deserved to know the worst. Striving to keep the fear out of her voice, she added, "We're waiting for the paramedics."

Brennermen stared at the burning barn and uttered the first curse Sarah had ever heard from his self-righteous lips. "You can wait. I'm going in."

The deputy held out a restraining hand. "Sir, you can't—"

Brennermen didn't even bother to answer. He shoved past the young man and ran toward the barn, determined as usual to have his own way. But he apparently hadn't counted on the deputy's sense of duty—or his youthful strength. The deputy dashed after Brennermen and caught him by the arm, calling over his equally young partner for assistance. Together the two men held back the struggling father.

"Let go of me, dammit," Brennermen cried, his polished veneer cracking in desperation. "My girl's in there!"

His anguished plea struck Sarah to the heart. Personally, she couldn't stand the man, but as a parent she couldn't help sharing his pain. She laid a comforting hand on his beefy forearm. "Look, Cathy's not in there alone. Luke went in after her."

She expected gratitude. Instead, Brennermen's eyes narrowed in contempt. "That saddle tramp?"

"That *tramp*," Sarah fired back, "is risking his life to save your child!"

Brennermen started to say something, but he was drowned out by a loud, groaning sound. The midsection of the roof was crumbling, sending a plume of sparks into the black sky. Sarah heard Brennermen gasp. She turned and saw her own helpless anguish mirrored in his eyes.

The sick fear she'd been holding off for so long flowed into her like an unstoppable torrent. *Please, God, don't let me lose him. I love him so much.*

"Hey," the young deputy said. "I think someone's coming out."

Sarah's desperate gaze flew toward the base of the barn. At first she saw only shifting flames and darkness, then one of the shadows began to form itself into a shape. A tall, lean shape carrying a smaller one . . .

Crying out, she ran hell-for-leather toward the barn. She ignored the shouts of the deputies. An army of deputies couldn't have stopped her at that moment. She flew like the wind, disregarding the waves of smoke and heat radiating from the barn. She didn't care. She had eyes only for the man who meant more to her than the hurts of her past and the uncertainties of her future. He was the man she loved and would continue to love until she drew her last breath.

A few seconds before she reached him, Luke set the girl he was carrying on her feet. Cathy sped past her into the waiting arms of her father, who'd apparently followed Sarah step for step. Sarah hardly spared a glance for the reunion of daughter and father. Her gaze was riveted on Luke. One leg of his jeans was ripped from his knee to his ankle, and his light shirt was streaked black with soot. His new hat was the sorriest sight of all, battered worse than his old one, and burned. He looked as though he had been through a war, but she'd never seen a more welcome sight.

"Luke," she cried as she ran into his open arms and buried her face against the hard reality of his chest. "You're all right. You're really all right."

He gave her his notorious cocksure grin. "Take more than a little fire to get the best of me."

His voice trembled a bit, but she took it for exhaustion. She wrapped her arms around him, hugging him with all her strength. He smelled of foul ash and caustic smoke, as if he'd been through the fires of hell. She breathed deeply, welcoming his scent more than the sweetest-smelling spring morning. "If anything had happened to you, I wouldn't want to live. I—my God, you're bleeding!"

"Just a scratch," Luke said, but the weakness in his voice belied his statement. So did the red stain spreading across the torn arm of his shirt.

Panicked, Sarah called out to the deputies, who came running on the double. They each took one of Luke's arms and lent him support as they walked him back to the car, although he grumbled the whole while that he didn't need their help. Sarah walked beside them, more and more distressed by the unnatural pallor of his skin. In the distance she heard the sharp wail of the approaching paramedics.

She prayed they'd get there in time.

"I'm fine," Luke stated for the third time in as many minutes. "Or I will be as soon as I get out of this place!"

The emergency-room physician, a competent man with the emotional range of a block of wood, acknowledged Luke's tirade with barely a sniff. "You'll leave when I say so," he said, calmly examining the bandage he'd secured over the five stitches he'd taken in Luke's upper arm. "And I want you back here in a week, so I can reexamine the wound and take out the stitches."

Luke gave the physician a dark look and mumbled something about "not needing to be coddled." He started to say more, but Sarah cut him off.

"He'll be here, Doctor," she assured him, "if I have to drag him here by his spurs."

Luke glanced over at her. She stood near the door with her arms folded in front of her, and a no-nonsense expression on her beautiful face. Luke sighed, knowing he was outgunned. "Okay," he promised curtly. "I'll come back. Just tell me how soon I can get the hell out of this place."

The doctor straightened and made a quick, final notation on his chart. "As soon as you want," he said as he headed out the door. "With any luck I will not be the attending physician when you return. I've rarely met a more obstinate patient."

"Little weasel," Luke muttered as he watched the doctor go. He grabbed up his shirt and started to pull it on.

"Oh, I don't know," Sarah said, coming over to help him. "I think his evaluation was pretty accurate. You're a terrible patient. I ought to know."

Yes, she surely ought to. Luke's mind went back to the night they met, when she'd tended his bruise. Despite his surly attitude she'd been gentle and caring, giving him his first glimpse of the tender, loving spirit beneath her bristly exterior. She was as loving now, helping him tug on the remains of his ruined shirt. Every move she made was precious to him. He caught her hand and placed a warm kiss on the base of her palm. "I like your doctoring much better," he said, his voice teasing. "Especially your *bed*side manner."

She blushed a pretty rose color that spoke both of pleasure and embarrassment. "You're incorrigible," she said, though her scolding lacked conviction. "And don't think you're going to sweet-talk me out of bringing you back here."

"Wouldn't dream of it," he lied. Then, in a lower, huskier tone, he added, "I guess that means I'll be staying on a few more days."

Her hands stilled on his collar. She lifted her gaze tentatively to meet his, a thousand questions in her expressive, bewitching eyes. Luke dearly wanted to take her in his arms and answer each of those thousand questions with a kiss, but he wasn't sure that kisses were the answers she needed. He'd have to wait until she asked her questions. He'd have to let her make the first move, even if it meant riding roughshod over every urge in his body. Dammit.

"Luke," she said quietly. "About what we were discussing. Before the fire, I mean—"

A sharp rap on the door curtailed her speech. *I'm gonna horsewhip that doctor*, Luke vowed. "What is it now, Doc?"

But it wasn't the doctor. Sam Brennermen stepped through the doorway, looking no happier to be there than Luke was to have him. Sarah disregarded the tension between them and immediately went over to Brennermen. "How's Cathy?" she asked with honest concern.

"She inhaled some smoke, but the doctor expects she'll be able to go home tomorrow. She's fine, thanks to"—Brennermen hemmed and hawed, clearing his throat a couple of times—"thanks to Mr. Tyrell."

Luke suspected Brennermen would rather swallow ground glass than thank him and smiled at the thought. However, he was genuinely relieved to hear the kid was going to be okay. "I'm glad I could get her out," he said honestly. "No one deserves that kind of fate, even if she was responsible for the fire."

Once again Brennermen cleared his throat. "Yes, about that. I was hoping we could keep that little matter between ourselves. After all, there's really no harm done—"

Luke stared at the smug, portly man, wondering if he was making some sort of bizarre joke. "*No harm?* Sarah's barn is in ashes. *I* was almost in ashes. If you think I'm forgetting about it, guess again."

Brennermen's eyes widened in surprise, but he quickly regained his composure. He reached into his pocket and pulled out a folded check, which he handed to Sarah. "I know you've experienced a great deal of inconvenience. Perhaps this will help make up for it."

Luke watched over Sarah's shoulder as she unfolded the check. It was written for an amount of money large enough to buy three barns. He watched her face grow sickly pale at the implied bribe.

His jaw clenched in anger. If Brennermen had tried to bribe a jaded character like himself, Luke might have forgiven him. But to insult the integrity of a woman as fine and true as Sarah . . . "I suggest you leave," Luke said, his voice packed with lethal menace. "Now."

"But about my daughter—"

"Hang your daughter," he stated angrily. "And hang you! Your money can't buy our silence. Cathy committed a crime, and she'll have to pay for it, like everyone else."

Brennermen's supercilious facade slipped, giving Luke a glimpse of the worried father underneath. "Please," he said, sounding sincere for the first time since he entered the room. "Cathy's never been in trouble before. She's got her whole life ahead of her. Don't let this one foolish act ruin her future."

Luke had no desire to ruin Cathy's future, but he dearly wanted to take a swipe at Brennermen's. The self-righteous jerk had made Sarah's life hell since she and her children had come to live at Corners. There was no doubt in Luke's mind that bringing Cathy up on charges would wound her father tenfold. He turned to Sarah, uncertain of what to do.

Sarah looked back at him, her eyes full of more trust than he'd ever dreamed possible. "You were the one who risked your life to save Cathy," she told him. "You decide."

Eight weeks ago Luke would have taken his revenge on Brennermen without giving the girl's fate a second thought. He'd lived a hard, cold life full of hard, cold realities. But loving Sarah and her kids had worked a profound change in him. He knew there was a truth beyond harsh justice. He knew that love and forgiveness could change the course of a person's life, no matter how black his sins.

He knew that, whether they deserved it or not, everyone needed a second chance.

Luke turned back to Brennermen, hoping that Sarah wouldn't think him a coward for backing down. "We won't press charges," he stated quietly. "Now get out."

Brennermen didn't have to be told twice. He opened the door but gave Luke a final, searching look just before he left. "You're a hard man to figure out, Tyrell."

"He's right, you know," Sarah said after the door

had clicked shut behind him. "You *are* a hard man to figure out."

Luke shoved his fingers through his hair in a quick, frustrated swipe. "I wanted that guy's blood so bad, I could taste it. But . . . I couldn't use his kid to get back at him. I know firsthand how a bad reputation can mess up a person's life. I'm sorry—" He paused, studying her eyes like a pirate trying to decipher a treasure map. "I'm sorry if that wasn't the way you wanted it."

"Luke, how can you even think that?" she asked, falling into his arms. The check fluttered to the ground, unheeded by them both. "Showing mercy to that girl took a lot more courage than seeking revenge. I didn't think it was possible to love you any more than I already do." She lifted her tear-bright gaze to his. "But I was wrong."

Luke looked at her in wonder. He'd never, never understand this woman, but it occurred to him that understanding her wasn't all that important. He lifted his hand to her face and traced the sweet outline of her generous, giving smile. "Do you think you love me enough to marry me?"

"I always have," she confessed, her breath feather soft against the tips of his fingers. "It was your memories of Annie that stopped me from saying yes."

"Annie? What's Annie got to do with you and me?"

"She was your first love. I know she'll always have first place in your heart, but I don't care anymore," she said, clinging to him with all her strength. "When the fire almost took you, I knew I couldn't bear living my life without you."

Luke stared at her in surprise. "You think Annie was my lover?"

"Of course. You dream about her. The tragedy of her loss has shaped your life."

"That's true," Luke said, cupping her face gently between his palms. "I'll always cherish Annie's memory. But she wasn't my lover, Sarah. She was my daughter."

THIRTEEN

The clock on the emergency-room wall whirred away the seconds. An overhead vent rattled slightly as the climate-controlled air rushed through it. Sarah heard the hushed, vaguely irregular sound of her breathing, and the deeper, rougher timbre of Luke's. It seemed every sound in the small room had been magnified to a deafening pitch, including the thumping of her own startled heart.

"Your daughter?" she repeated.

Luke sighed, his broad shoulders bent under a weariness greater than she'd ever seen in him before. "It was years ago. It's a long story."

"I'm not going anywhere," she said quietly.

He looked at her, his lips curved in a smile so sweet and sad, it made her heart ache. He covered her slim hand with his broad one, lacing their fingers together in a firm bond. "I know. But I haven't told this to anyone in a while. You'll have to bear with me."

She nodded, too full of emotion to speak. He was finally going to trust her with his past. With Annie. She sat down on the examination table beside him and waited for him to begin.

"I grew up on a ranch out in West Texas, in a county so sparsely populated, it makes this one look like Dallas Central. The work was honest, but hard. Sometimes my parents and I would go weeks without seeing anyone. Mom handled my schooling—she was a teacher before she met Dad—but I never had much to do with other kids until I was in my teens."

"It must have been a lonely life," Sarah commented.

"Sometimes," he agreed. "But not often. I had all the farm animals for friends, and the rocky cliffs, and the wide blue sky. I was alone a lot of the time, but I wasn't lonely, if you know what I mean."

Sarah did know. As a child who hadn't quite fit in with her proper, upper-class family, she'd spent a great deal of time on her own. "Sometimes you can be more alone in a crowd than you can ever be by yourself."

Luke's grip on her hand tightened. "I found that out. When I was in my early teens, we had a couple of drought years, and Dad had to sell out. We moved east and worked rented land. I went to the county high school, but I still kept pretty much to myself. Until I saw Tess, that is."

Tess. He spoke the name with uncertain reverence, like a man showing off a family heirloom that has long since ceased to be of any practical use.

"Your wife?" Sarah asked.

Luke nodded. "She was a pretty thing, bright as the tinsel on a Christmas tree. All the boys courted her, but I was the one she said yes to. We were married the summer after we graduated from high school.

"Almost from the start we knew it was a mistake. Tess was used to being the belle of the ball. She wanted fun and excitement, but as a part-time college student working full time to make ends meet, I didn't have much time for either. I wanted to learn all I could about the newest agricultural methods, so I'd be better prepared to make it through the bad-weather years that forced Dad under. Tess took a few classes here and there, but she wasn't really interested in getting an education. Truthfully, I don't think she ever understood why *I* was interested in getting one."

Sarah thought back to her own failed relationship. "You both wanted different things out of life," she said, speaking almost more to herself than to him.

"She sure didn't want the simple kind of life I did," he commented harshly. "She wanted me to quit school and get a job that paid better, like some of our high school classmates, the guys she had turned down, were doing. We argued all the time. For two years it seemed to me that the only conversations we had were at the top of our lungs. All the love we'd felt for each other soured into bitter regret. Finally, we decided to call it quits. Then . . ."

"Tess got pregnant," Sarah said hollowly.

Again Luke nodded. "To her credit, Tess really tried to make it work after she found out. We *both* did. We'd grown up in stable, loving families, and we wanted our kid to have the same kind of childhood. But it didn't last. Money became even tighter, and Tess couldn't understand why I wouldn't give up college to give our child a better life. We argued even more. I hated what I'd done to the bright, happy girl I'd married, but I couldn't change, any more than she could. I was miserable. I thought nothing could bring joy back to my life—until the moment I held Annie in my arms."

His smile faltered as his sight focused inward on his old, bitter memories. Sarah felt his pain as if it were her own. "You don't have to go on," she told him.

"No. I want to." He clasped his free hand over their joined ones, as if drawing comfort from the bond. "I want you to know all of it." He drew a deep breath and continued.

"It was love at first sight for me. I know every father thinks his little girl is special, but Annie—she was truly rare. She was bursting with love for the whole crazy world, and somehow she made me love it too. No matter how bad things got between Tess and me, Annie could always make it better with a hug and a smile. At least with me she could."

"But not with Tess," Sarah offered.

Luke shook his head. "Don't get me wrong—Tess loved Annie. But she wasn't much more than a kid herself. She still craved the excitement of the single life, and Annie and I hung like stones around her neck. Looking back, I can see that the guilt must have been eating her up inside. But at the time, all I knew was that she hated me and the life I'd given her. We didn't have any kind of a marriage anymore. We didn't even argue.

"My part-time classes were finally adding up to a degree. But as graduation approached, I had to give even more time to my studies, sometimes spending whole nights in the library. I told myself that once I'd graduated, I'd make it up to Tess and really work on our marriage for Annie's sake. But it didn't turn out that way. One night a fellow classmate warned me that he'd seen my wife at another man's house. The guy had a reputation as a rounder. I knew he'd been after Tess for months—along with most of the other married women in town. Marital problems or not, she was still my wife."

The hard line of Luke's jaw tightened almost imperceptibly, telling Sarah more about his remembered anguish than words ever could. She was in conflict: She wanted to tell him to stop, that she couldn't bear to see him in this kind of pain, but she knew she had to let him continue. Talking about his past was the only way he was going to get over it. She had to help him through it. "Did you go to the man's house?"

He gave a short, bitter laugh. "Yeah, I went. She was . . . well, you can imagine. Finding Tess with another man was bad enough, but the thing that really made my blood boil was, she'd brought

Annie along, because the sitter had canceled. I couldn't believe she'd expose our daughter to something like that, even young as she was. I packed them both up into the truck and drove off without a word. The guy was only too glad to see the back of us.

"I was furious. Tess was furious and embarrassed. From the guy's cowardly reaction she knew she'd made a fool of herself. We argued all the way home, but at least we were talking to each other again. The things she said made me realize how abandoned she'd felt by my nights away from home. She even thought *I* was having an affair. She was so relieved when I told her I wasn't that I realized she still had feelings for me. I began to think we might be able to make our marriage work after all.

"Annie was asleep in the back of the cab. We'd tried to keep our voices low, but she heard us and woke up crying. I turned around to comfort her. My eyes were off the road for two, maybe three, seconds—"

"Oh God," Sarah said weakly. "An accident."

"A drunk driver," Luke said, his words echoing hollowly in the room. "One minute I was in my truck with my family. The next I was waking up in a hospital bed with a broken leg and collarbone. The doctors didn't have to tell me Tess and Annie didn't make it. I saw it on their faces."

Sarah tightened her grip on his hand. "You weren't responsible. It was the other driver."

"Responsible or not, they were gone," he stated.

"In a single instant everyone I loved was just . . . not there. Losing Tess was bad enough, but losing my Annie was past bearing. All my education, all the dreams I had and the plans I made—none of them could bring Annie back to me. I hated the fact that she'd died while I'd survived with only a few minor injuries. I hated it more because there was nothing at all I could do about it. I felt I didn't have any control over my life. It suddenly seemed a cruel, pointless joke.

"I quit school and went from job to job, working enough to make ends meet. I'd been on my own a lot as a kid, and I found it easy to fall back into my old loner ways. Sometimes I'd find a woman I thought I could care about, but I'd always end up remembering about Tess and Annie. It was easier to move on than to get involved. Eventually, I started avoiding anyone I had even an inkling I might be able to care about."

"You didn't avoid us," Sarah said quietly.

"That's true," Luke said, smiling for the first time in many minutes. "But who'd have thought I'd come to care for a crazy woman and her five little hellraisers?"

"I'm not crazy."

Luke's smile broadened into a rakish grin. Laugh lines crinkled at the corners of his eyes, making his intense gaze even more seductive. "You're crazy as a bedbug. Otherwise you wouldn't have gotten within spitting distance of an outlaw like me."

Sarah started to say that he wasn't an outlaw, but she never finished her sentence. Quicker than she'd believed possible for an injured man, Luke pulled her onto his lap and folded her against his chest, consuming her with a deep, hungry kiss. Love blazed through her, love for this good, noble man who'd lost so much in his life. She ached to heal him, to give him a bright, splendid future free from the troubles of the past. But her intrinsic honesty made her realize a trouble-free life wasn't hers to promise.

"Luke," she murmured as he held her against his chest, "there still aren't any guarantees. I love you. Always. But I can't promise you that an accident won't happen—"

His strong arms crushed her against him. "I know," he said roughly. "But I was wrong to mourn Annie. I wasted years regretting losing her, when I should have been thankful for the time we had together." He rested his cheek against her hair and breathed a sigh so deep, it seemed to come from the center of his soul. "Life is too precious to waste on regrets. *You're* too precious."

Tears filled her eyes. She lifted her gaze to meet his and saw more love than she'd dreamed possible burning in his sky-blue eyes. "You know, cowboy," she said shakily, "you would make one hell of a lawyer."

"Naw. Too much arguing." His eyes took on a devilish gleam. "I prefer other forms of persuasion."

He dipped his head to give her a firsthand taste of one of those forms, when he was halted by a knock on the door. "That doctor is buzzard bait," he growled.

Sarah started to shift off his lap, inwardly echoing the sentiment. "Wait a minute," she called.

The door opened immediately, admitting not the doctor, but Rafe. "Hey, I found them," he yelled down the hall behind him. Then, after a second look, he added, "He's okay. They're necking."

Sarah blushed furiously at Rafe's loud announcement. Luke chuckled. Shooting him a dark look, Sarah got to her feet. Seeing her and Luke together would be an incredible shock for Rafe, and for all her children. She'd have to break the news of their impending marriage to them very gently, tactfully—

"We're getting hitched," Luke stated as soon as her assorted kids had gathered in the room.

So much for tact. "Kids," Sarah explained. "This isn't as sudden as it seems. Luke and I have been, uh, seeing each other for the past few weeks."

Jenny shrugged her shoulders. "We figured. We know you've been sleeping together."

Sarah's jaw dropped. "How . . . how did you know?"

Micah stopped his absorbing examination of Luke's bandaged arm to answer. "You always walked past my door when you went downstairs and out to the tack room. The first night I woke everyone up, and we had a conference. We decided it was okay, since it was Luke. How many stitches did they take?"

"Five," Luke answered, trying unsuccessfully to hide his smile. "And thanks for the vote of confidence."

Micah's shrug mirrored Jenny's. "It was a break for us. We were trying to come up with ways to get you to stay, Luke. We figured Sarah was our best bet."

"Though we had backup plans," Rafe assured him.

"Pooling our allowances to pay you more," Lyn said.

"Hiding your belongings so you'd think someone stole them," Jenny offered.

"Taking the keys to your truck," Valerie added enthusiastically. "We were going to sew them inside Mr. Bear."

Sarah looked at each of her little reprobates. They were proud of their schemes. "Kids," she said, mortified. "You shouldn't even be thinking such things. You can't make another person's decisions for him."

"Why not," Jenny asked, "if they're the right decisions?"

"No mistakes there, Spots," Rafe agreed, in what had to be a first. "We knew Luke didn't really want to leave us. We only had to make sure he stuck around until he figured it out for himself."

Feeling outnumbered, Sarah glanced at Luke for help. He smiled back at her with barely contained laughter. Belatedly, Sarah realized she had her work cut out for her. She didn't have just one outlaw. She had a whole band of them.

"I give up," she said, laughing. "I know when I'm outnumbered. But we still need to get home. It's the middle of the night, and you guys have school tomorrow."

Various and assorted grumbles met her announcement. "None of that," she cautioned. "Besides, Luke needs to get some rest."

The gleam in Luke's eyes told her that *rest* was the last thing he intended to get tonight. Still, he dutifully kept that thought to himself. "We should all be getting back to Corners. After all, it's going to be a big day tomorrow, with the inspection and all."

The inspection! In the excitement of the fire and Luke's injury, she'd forgotten about it. "We're not ready," she said, suddenly panicked. "What'll they say about the fire, the barn?"

Luke rose from the examination table and slipped his good arm around her shoulders. "They'll say we were damn lucky," he told her. Then, bending close to her ear, he added, "and they won't know the half of it."

Sarah knew what he meant. She and Luke not only had survived the fire, but also found a love that was real and true enough to build a future on. As she watched Luke good-naturedly herd the kids from the room, she caught a glimpse of what that future would be. Five unruly children and a former drifter might not seem like much to most people, but she would have cut out her heart before she'd have parted with a single one of them. Seven wandering souls had come together to make a family, a family joined by trust and love, strong enough to weather the storms of the future. Her heart swelled with bright joy, diminished only by one dark uncertainty.

Lord, what was the inspector going to say about the barn?

FOURTEEN

"Oh no, it's worse than I thought," Sarah said, peering through the living-room window. "He's brought *her* with him."

Luke bent over Sarah's shoulder and looked through the opening she'd made in the curtains. "Her who?"

"Mrs. Graves," Sarah said weakly, pointing toward the woman getting out of the building inspector's car. Of all the people she'd expected to see today, Amanda Graves was the one she least expected—and least welcomed. "She's the children's social worker from Dallas."

Luke squinted as he took a closer look at the woman. "Shoot, she's just a little bit of a thing. Sort of reminds me of my grandmother."

Sarah let the curtain fall back into place, then turned around to face him, her expression full of real distress. "Don't let her age fool you. She's notorious. She's strictly by the book, a stickler for detail. And"— she lowered her voice to a shaky whisper—"she has the complete authority to revoke my application for adoption if we don't pass the inspection."

Luke took her gently by the shoulders. "She's not going to revoke anything. We've worked hard to get this place in shape. We'll pass the inspection."

"But what if—"

"But nothin'. No one is going to take those kids away from you, Sarah. Not while there's breath in my body. That's a promise. Besides," he added, "I'm pretty *notorious* myself when it comes to charming the ladies."

Despite her anxiety, Sarah couldn't help smiling. "Oh, you are—"

"Incorrigible. I know."

Their gazes locked, and she felt his love pour through her like warm, bright sunshine. She drew on his strength and the sweet certainty of their love. With Luke by my side I can face anything, she thought. Even Mrs. Graves. "Okay, cowboy. Let's get this party started."

"Yes, ma'am."

He gave her shoulders a reassuring squeeze, then released her and headed to the front door. She followed a pace behind, watching his sure and easy stride, taking pride in his confident manner. She loved him fiercely, now more than ever.

A moment ago when their gazes had met, she'd

seen something in the depth of his eyes, a subtle emotion she'd never have noticed if she hadn't known him so well. She'd spotted a flicker of doubt, a shadow of concern, quickly concealed. Underneath all his bluster and bravado he was as nervous as she.

They had good reason to be concerned. Hank Rearden, the building inspector, shook their hands with cool professionalism, but Mrs. Graves's greeting was positively frigid. The petite woman wore an expression that would have soured milk, and her crisp gray suit looked as if it had just left the ironing board. Probably a wrinkle wouldn't dare crease her skirt, Sarah thought with the ghost of a smile.

Mrs. Graves's quick eye caught Sarah's faint grin and frowned in disapproval. She perused both Luke and Sarah with a sharp, penetrating glance. She might have been making a cursory inventory of all their obvious defects. Under that subzero stare Sarah felt her temperature drop ten degrees, but it was Luke who bore the brunt of it.

"I've done some checking into your background, Mr. Tyrell," she said in a voice stiff enough to starch a shirt. "Most particularly into that incident in Abilene."

Luke's cavalier smile died. "That was years ago."

"Four years and five months to be precise," Mrs. Graves stated. She flipped open the thick folder she carried and studied one of the pages. "According to this, you and the rest of your crew were shown out of town by a police escort. The incident hardly makes you an ideal role model for impressionable children.

However, I must admit that your work record is exemplary."

"Uh, thanks, I think," Luke said, clearly unsure of what to make of the woman.

"No need to thank me for stating the facts, young man," she commented briskly. She snapped the folder shut and took an abbreviated look at her watch. "Mr. Rearden, we're already running late for this inspection. I believe we should start with the house. . . ."

Still talking at a breakneck clip, she walked off with the wisely quiet Mr. Rearden. Sarah and Luke followed a yard behind. "I did warn you," Sarah remarked.

"You did," Luke acknowledged, tipping back the brim of his old hat. "But I doubt whether a hundred warnings could have prepared me for the likes of Mrs. Graves. That lady bears watching. I haven't been sucker-punched like that since . . . well, since Abilene."

"What happened?"

Luke shook his head. "I was a damn fool, that's what happened. A man had something I wanted, and I fought him for it. Of course the man was twice as big as I was, and about half as drunk. My crew stepped in to help me out, and pretty soon the whole bar was brawling."

"Sounds like quite a fight," Sarah commented as she lengthened her steps to match his long-legged stride. "Was she pretty?"

"Who?"

She smiled knowingly at Luke. "The woman you were fighting over, of course."

Luke turned sharply, clearly surprised that she'd figured everything out so quickly. Then his mouth pulled up in a sheepish, endearing grin. "She couldn't hold a candle to you, darlin'."

He'd meant to laugh off the event, but Sarah knew him well enough to hear the underlying worry in his tone. "Luke," she said, her voice too low for anyone but him to hear, "whatever Mrs. Graves says, the past doesn't matter. We've got a wonderful future ahead of us, cowboy, and don't you forget it."

He glanced at her briefly, the naked desire in his eyes making her heart turn a somersault in her chest. Then he hurried on to catch up with the two before they reached the porch. Sarah followed at a slower pace, using the extra seconds to rein in her galloping emotions. She had to keep her mind focused on passing the inspection, and off her love for Luke. Otherwise, she'd never be able to stop herself from telling the judgmental Mrs. Graves exactly what she thought of her.

Sarah managed to keep her temper under control for the rest of the inspection. Her spirits were another matter. True, she and Luke had made the necessary repairs to the house, and the animals were all well-tended and cared for, but no matter how hard she tried to avoid it, her gaze was always drawn back to the blackened ruin of her barn. Rearden and Mrs. Graves had noticed the barn, too, but so far neither had commented on it. *Saving the worst for last*, she thought glumly.

What would happen if they didn't pass the inspection? Once the thought had filled her with an almost paralyzing terror, but suddenly she found herself able to face that possibility without fear. If they didn't pass, Luke and she would pack up the kids and move somewhere else. Home wasn't a place; it was wherever her family was. It was as simple, and as profound, as that.

She loved Corners, but looking back, she realized she'd fought leaving it because she wanted to prove something to her family and, as much as she hated to admit it, to Paul. She wanted them to see that she could make a life for herself and her kids despite their disapproval. Leaving Corners would have meant that she'd failed. I was still living my life for them, she realized. Until Luke showed me how to believe in myself, I was still living for them.

Her thoughts ended abruptly as Hank Rearden's shadow fell across her. "Miss Gallagher," he said as he came to stand in front of her. "We'll be finished here in a few minutes."

"Take your time," Sarah said, smiling wryly. She felt like a condemned criminal telling the hangman not to rush with the noose. Oddly, she didn't mind the execution nearly as much as she thought she would. She glanced around for Luke and caught sight of him leaning against the porch post. His stance was deceptively lazy; his expression was intense while he watched Mrs. Graves examine the repairs he'd made to the front steps. He was a good distance away;

nevertheless, when he lifted his gaze to meet Sarah's, something living crackled between them. Almost a barnyard away, he still stopped her breath with his intensity.

"Miss Gallagher?"

Sarah turned and caught sight of Rearden looking at her with vague concern. Damn. He'd probably said something, and she'd missed it entirely. "Sorry," she said, hoping she didn't sound as breathless as she felt. "Did you ask me something?"

The inspector nodded. "Yes. I have a few questions to ask you about your barn."

Here it comes, she thought. She pulled her shoulders straighter, instinctively tensing for battle, even though she knew it wouldn't do her a bit of good. Reading people had been her business for years, and she could tell by the set of Rearden's jaw that he'd already made up his mind. "What would you like to know?"

"Is the structure salvageable?"

Sarah looked over at the ruins. The scorched timbers rose up like the bones of some prehistoric animal, the charred remains of a giant's dinner. The fire department had arrived in the eleventh hour and managed to save the far end of the barn and the tack room from total destruction. But as she looked at the gaunt, blackened structure, Sarah couldn't help wishing they'd put the sorry thing out of its misery and let it burn to the ground. "No, Mr. Rearden. It is definitely not salvageable."

The inspector jotted a note on his clipboard. "Are you planning to rebuild?"

Like I'm going to get the chance, she thought bleakly. With effort she bit back the caustic response she dearly wanted to give. "I'd very much like to."

"Uhmm," Rearden said cryptically as he jotted down another note. He put the clipboard under his arm and started to walk away.

Having Rearden turn his back on her was the last straw. "Hey," she said, walking after him. When he didn't stop, she cut in front of him, blocking his path. "Okay, I'm tired of playing games."

Rearden blinked at her as though she had a screw loose. "Excuse me?"

"Give it to me straight," she said with a great deal more confidence than she felt. "I want to know if I passed the inspection."

"What's all this?" Mrs. Graves asked as she hustled over to Rearden's side.

The inspector looked at her with an affronted expression. "Miss Gallagher wants to know if she passed. But it's standard procedure not to give a definite answer until we've discussed it between ourselves—"

"So discuss it," a deep voice interrupted. Luke approached the group and immediately took a protective stance beside Sarah. "You've kept Miss Gallagher on tenterhooks for months over this. She's worked like hell to get this place in shape, despite"—he added, giving Rearden, who was Brennermen's brother-in-law, a meaningful glare—"despite repeated roadblocks from the community and a fire that almost claimed the life of your niece. Let Miss Gallagher know where she stands. She's more than earned the right."

Neither Mrs. Graves nor Rearden looked especially pleased by Luke's effrontery, but they went back to the porch and compared their notes, talking the matter over in hushed tones. Sarah strained to hear, but the wind carried away their words. Old memories came back of courtrooms and jury trials and people she didn't know deciding the fate of her clients. Only this time she was the client. And the scaled-down judge and jury were in Brennermen's back pocket.

She turned to the man beside her, looking up into his beloved, worried face. "Luke, if we don't pass—"

"We will," he stated gruffly, his jaw tightening. "Even if I have to hog-tie the both of them."

Sarah couldn't resist a smile. Luke's sense of justice was about as subtle as a Texas cyclone, and she loved him for it. She brushed her hand across the rigid line of his cheek, gentling him with her touch. "If we don't pass," she continued, "we'll just find someplace else to live. Corners is only a house. You and the kids are my home."

Her quiet words sent a tremor through him. His bold gaze caught hers, melting her with the fierce tenderness she'd experienced so many times in the midst of their lovemaking. "Woman," he mused, "if I live to be a hundred, I'm never gonna figure you out."

"Miss Gallagher?"

Reluctantly, Sarah looked from Luke to Rearden,

who approached her, a folded slip of paper in his hand. *Ladies and gentlemen of the jury, have you reached a verdict?*

He handed her the paper. She stared at the innocent-looking slip, and found herself incapable of unfolding it. "Luke, could you . . . ?"

She didn't even have to finish her sentence. He took the paper from her hand, opened it, and grimly studied the contents. She watched him closely for a change in his expression. She saw none, until he stopped reading and met her eyes. He's stunned, she thought.

"Sarah," he said, his voice as unsteady as a newborn colt, "you passed."

Passed. For a moment they could do nothing but stare at each other, letting the reality sink in. Then Luke let out a holler to wake the dead and wrapped her in his arms, swinging her around in a tremendous bear hug. "We did it, Sarah," he cried. "We really did it!"

She tried to answer, but laughter and tears got in the way of her words. They'd passed the inspection. Together they'd beaten the odds, turning the run-down farm into a livable home. Our home, she thought with a joy so huge, it felt as if it would burst her heart. Together they would build a new life here, free from the ghosts of their past. Passing the inspection wasn't the only way they'd beaten the odds.

Luke set her down. She clung to his broad shoulders, still caught between laughter and tears, and started to mouth the words she hadn't the breath to say. "I love y—"

"Miss Gallagher," Mrs. Graves interrupted, appearing suddenly at their sides. "I'd like to congratulate you on an exemplary job. And you too, Mr. Tyrell," she said with a concessionary nod. "Your personal record leaves much to be desired, but as an employee you are quite adequate. I would not object if Miss Gallagher considered keeping you on until—"

"Miss Gallagher's considered doing a sight more than just keeping me on," he said, enveloping Sarah in another wholehearted hug. "She's agreed to marry me."

Rearden's jaw dropped, and Mrs. Graves's eyes widened in totally uncharacteristic surprise. "Marry you?"

"That's right," Luke said, his smile mellowing as he turned his gaze back to Sarah. "She's a smart lady. Now she and the kids will have free hired help for the rest of their lives."

"Not so free, cowboy," Sarah said, playfully punching him in the ribs. "I still have to feed you."

"Among other things," he murmured, his grin turning wicked.

Sarah blushed, pleased and embarrassed by the raw intimacy in Luke's glance. But what would the others think? Probably that we've been doing exactly what we've been doing, she realized, and colored even more deeply at the thought. She cast an apologetic look at

Mrs. Graves, and met a pair of eyes as shockingly cold as ice water.

"Miss Gallagher," the older woman said in a voice that matched her expression. "I must talk to you. In private."

In other words, without Luke. Mrs. Graves still considered him to be a second-class citizen, as Brennermen and so many others had. Sarah sighed in exasperation. They never took the trouble to look beneath his drifter image to the strong, courageous, and compassionate person. He was worth a hundred Brennermens. A hundred hundred. And no one was going to treat him like an outcast, not while she was around.

She firmly grasped Luke's hand and drew herself up to her full height, facing the older woman with an icy expression of her own. "If you have something to say, I'd rather you say it in front of my fiancé."

"As you wish," Mrs. Graves said. She continued, her knife-edged words cutting straight to the point. "Mr. Tyrell's reputation is questionable at best, and I have serious reservations about his character. As a temporary employee his damaging influence on the children could be kept to a minimum, but as a husband and father—"

"As a husband and father he'd be wonderful!" Sarah cried, her temper rising. "The children are crazy about him."

"Sarah—" Luke warned.

"I don't care," she told him. "I'm tired of everyone treating you like you're something the cat dragged in.

I love you. And I'm going to marry you"—she shot a baleful glance at Mrs. Graves—"in spite of other people's reservations."

Mrs. Graves met her gaze with the rigid, uncompromising judgment of blindfolded Justice. "I certainly can't stop you from marrying him," she agreed succinctly. "But if you do, I'll have to reevaluate your competency as an adoptive parent."

FIFTEEN

Evening stole across the land. Sweet, fragrant flowers gave their scent to the unhurried breeze, and the setting sun burnished the wide horizon in a soft, glowing shade of rose. The world seemed cool and peaceful, blessed with a twilight grace that made everyone forget the troubles of the day and look forward to the promise of tomorrow. Everyone, that is, except the man who sat alone on the porch swing, absently fingering the brim of his Stetson. Tomorrow held no promise for him, and the evening meant nothing but the end of a dream.

The screen door opened, its screech tearing at the peace of the night. Luke didn't look up, knowing it was Sarah before she even stepped on the porch. He would always know when she was near. His inner self would continue to reach out to her, searching for her, even when he knew there was nothing left to find.

Grimly, he molded his face into a stoic mask. "Did you tell the kids?"

"Yes."

He heard the anguish in her voice, the hollow desolation that came with the death of a dream. Holding his emotions in a tight grip, he stood up and brushed some nonexistent dirt from his jeans. "Well, then, I guess that's it."

"No, it's not. You don't have to do this."

"Sarah—"

"Just hear me out," she said, coming to stand by his side. She didn't touch him—they'd agreed earlier that that would make their parting next to impossible— but the love in her eyes caressed him in ways her hands never could. "We can fight this. I'm a lawyer. I can challenge Mrs. Graves legally and build a case for your defense. In time we might be able to win a decision in your favor—"

"And lose your kids in the process," he stated harshly. He hated like hell to destroy her dreams, but it was the only way. Halfway hope was worse on a body than no hope at all. "Besides, it's not the law that's in question. It's my character. And all the wishing in the world won't make my record go away."

Sarah had no answer for that. Instead, she wrapped her arms tightly around her chest and turned her face to the dying light. "Remember the last time we stood here like this?" she asked in a voice as hushed as the wind. "It's hard to believe it was only last night."

It was impossible not to remember. He'd asked her to marry him on this very spot. They'd planned to spend the rest of their lives together. They'd gotten less than twenty-four hours. Regret for the life they'd never have welled up inside him, and he uttered a low curse. "Stop it, Sarah. You're only making this harder."

She kept her gaze on the sunset. "I'm sorry. I know what you're saying is right. I can't risk losing my kids. But I don't . . ." Her voice broke with emotion. "Dammit, Luke, I don't want to lose you, either."

"Sarah, we can't . . . oh, hell." Ignoring their agreement, he pulled her roughly into his arms, burying his face in the silky darkness of her hair.

She trembled against him, and the tears she'd been fighting against all afternoon finally started to flow. "I can't bear this," she whispered. "I thought I could, but I can't."

He held her tightly, as if his arms alone could protect her from the anguish she was feeling. It was useless, of course. She was as broken-up inside as he was. Suddenly, he wished that he'd never come here, that he'd never fallen in love with her and never caused her this pain. His life had been an empty road, going nowhere. But at least he wouldn't have had her tears on his conscience.

He heard the screen door open again. He watched the children come out on the porch, grim as if in a funeral procession. Rafe spoke for the solemn group, since he was the only one who didn't seem to be on the verge of tears. His gray eyes met Luke's with an understanding that far exceeded his years. "We wanted to say good-bye."

Sarah hastily wiped the tears from her eyes and stepped away from Luke, allowing the children their moment with him. One by one they came up and shook his hand. Lyn and Jenny tried to say something, but their words got caught in their throats. Even Micah was speechless.

Finally, it was Valerie's turn. Luke bent down and extended his hand to the little girl, but she didn't take it. Instead, she wrapped her arms around his legs and hugged him with all the strength in her small body. "Don't go, Luke. Please don't go."

Wordlessly, Luke untangled her arms and picked her up, cradling her against him. He'd thought that losing Annie would be the hardest thing he'd ever have to face in his life, but he'd been wrong. Leaving Sarah and her children was as bad. He lifted his gaze to the darkening heavens, where the bright stars were winking into existence. *Lord, just once can't You give me a break?*

Other lights caught his eyes. They shone from between the thick pines that bordered Sarah's property. Headlights. Cars were coming down the long drive that led to Corners. Lots of them.

"What the . . . ?" Luke turned to Sarah and saw his own surprise mirrored on her face. She didn't know what was going on either. He set Valerie on her feet and walked slowly down the porch steps. Cars and trucks began to pull into the yard, parking on the driveway, the front lawn, and in one case the flower bed. Luke tipped back his Stetson and stared at the assembly, counting more than a dozen cars with more on the way. People began to get out. Some, like Mrs. Kochakian, the school principal, he recognized. Most he didn't.

He felt Sarah come to his side, standing on the higher step behind him. "Look," she said, pointing toward a nearby couple, "that's Becky's parents. And Jill's mom is right behind them."

"Cathy's friends?" Luke asked. "What are they doing here?"

"I don't know," she answered, sounding worried. "You don't think they're here to throw us out, do you?"

"If they are, they'll have one hell of a fight on their hands," he promised. He crossed his hands across his chest, looking as immovable as a mountain. "Why don't one of you folks tell us what's going on here?"

"Be glad to, Mr. Tyrell," a familiar voice bellowed.

Stunned, Luke watched as Sam Brennermen worked his way to the front of the crowd. Cathy walked beside him, looking slightly bored but none the worse for her recent brush with death. But it was the other person Brennermen had in tow who literally made Luke's jaw drop open in surprise. "Mrs. Graves?"

"Humph," she sniffed, extracting her hand out of Brennermen's grasp. "I was on my way to the airport when the sheriff pulled me over and made me get into the car with this man. Apparently, Mr. Rearden had called and told him that you were leaving, Mr. Tyrell."

"That's what brothers-in-law are for," Brennermen said, looking very pleased with himself.

Mrs. Graves gave him a sour glare. "I was kidnapped, Mr. Tyrell, and brought here. And I understand it's all because of you."

"Me?" Luke said gruffly. "What's this got to do with me?"

Mrs. Graves pursed her lips into an annoying frown. "Mr. Brennermen told me the people of the community didn't want you to leave, that they were behind you, in spite of your past record." Her expression softened slightly as she looked around at the large assembly filling the front yard and the driveway beyond. "I must say it's an impressive show of support."

Sarah's hand gripped Luke's shoulder. "They're here because they want Luke to stay?"

"Don't look so shocked." Brennermen snorted. "Luke's the hero of the county. He saved my daughter's life—in more ways than one," he added, giving Luke a meaningful look. "I've got my faults, Tyrell, but I pay my debts. I figure," he added, as he turned to view the gathered throng, "this makes us even."

Luke stared at the crowd, at the dozens of people who had rallied to his defense. He had no doubt that Brennermen had strong-armed a couple of them, probably more than a couple, but certainly not all. The majority of them had come of their own free will to help him out, just neighbors doing for one of their own. *One of their own.*

Mrs. Graves cleared her throat. "Well," she remarked, "in light of this overwhelming support I feel it is only fair that I reconsider my decision. Mr. Tyrell, if the people of this community are willing to overlook your past, I believe I must do the same. If you wish to stay on here at Corners, I won't prevent you. However," she added, her mouth twitching in the barest hint of a smile, "the final decision is really up to Miss Gallagher."

Luke cocked his head toward Sarah. "What do you say, Miss Gallagher?"

Sarah's eyes were bright with tears, but this time from happiness. "I don't know," she said, grinning. "What do you say, kids? Should we take on this disreputable character?"

Their resounding yes shook the sky.

Sarah started to say something else, but she never got the chance. Luke swept her into his arms and sealed their bargain with a very thorough kiss. People clapped, car horns blared, and many shouted congratulations to the happy couple in pleasant, disorganized pandemonium.

Mrs. Graves stood on the edge of the frivolity, watching the general hubbub with a vague look of disapproval. She opened her satchel and used the glow of a nearby headlight to make a final note in her folder.

"I don't see what all the fuss is about." She sniffed. "After all, I was only stating the facts."

Silver waves lapped the pale sand of the Galveston beach. A sea gull skimmed low over the water, gliding soundlessly through the misty morning air. Gulf breezes, heavy with salt and summer, whispered past the condominium balcony and sliding glass door, and brushed like cool silk across the hot skin of the resting lovers. Luke yawned lazily and threaded his fingers through Sarah's hair, his only covering at the moment. "I guess I ought to give you your wedding present."

His bride smiled wickedly. "I thought you just gave it to me."

Soft laughter rumbled in his chest. "You are incorrigible," he said, borrowing her favorite expression. Sighing reluctantly, he pulled himself out of the wonderful tangle of Sarah's embrace and disappeared into the living room.

Stretching leisurely, Sarah sat up and pushed the heavy fall of hair away from her face. She looked at the thoroughly disheveled covers and blushed when she remembered all the things she and Luke had done to each other to get them into this condition. By rights they should be exhausted, but Sarah had never felt more energetic. She looked at the glass door. The silver dawn might have been newly minted just for her. Drawn by the light, she left the bed and wrapped a shawl around her nakedness, then stepped out onto the balcony.

The air still carried the remembered chill of the previous night, but Sarah scarcely noticed. Luke's cherishing love had warmed her soul, and she doubted that she would ever be truly cold again. She looked at the plain band of gold on her finger, strong enough to stand the test of time. A soft smile touched her lips. Millionaires and potentates could have their riches— this one gold ring made her the wealthiest woman in the world.

She felt him come up behind her. He circled her with his arm and pulled her back against the hard-packed expanse of his chest. "For a second I thought you'd left me," he said.

"Never." She rubbed the side of her cheek against his rough, musky pelt. "Besides, you promised me a present."

"I did," he agreed in his deep, resonating baritone. He placed a wallet-size photograph case in her hand. "My parents kept this for me. I wanted you to have it."

Intrigued, Sarah unfastened the clasp and opened the case. Inside was a picture of a little blond-haired girl with sky-blue eyes whose crooked smile was as familiar to Sarah as her own. She glanced up at Luke in surprise. "It's Annie, isn't it?"

He nodded. His smile was slightly sad, but free

from its former bitterness. Sarah knew that he still missed Annie and always would, but the tearing wound of her death had healed to a livable sorrow. She blinked back sudden tears, overwhelmed by the change in him and her part in it. Her love had given him the strength to let go of his past and move on. She breathed in the fresh salt air, feeling as if she were breathing in the dawn itself. It was time to put the past behind them, she decided. Entirely.

"I wonder," she said softly, "what our baby will look like?"

It took a moment for her words to sink in. When they did, Luke spun her around, grasping her shoulders as his surprised eyes searched hers. "*Our* baby?" he whispered.

"Don't look so shocked, cowboy," she said, laughing. "It happens."

"But when? I was always careful to protect you."

Green mischief danced in Sarah's eyes. "Well, as near as I can tell, it happened the day I threatened to dunk your hat in the trough—"

"And got us dunked instead," Luke finished. He shook his head in profound wonder. "Seems I owe that old hat of mine a debt of gratitude."

"Then you're happy about this?"

"Happy?" Luke replied as he pulled her against him in a tremendous bear hug. "I feel like I've cornered the market on happiness! Life's so damn good for us, I feel sorry for the rest of the people in this world. It doesn't seem fair."

Sarah reached up and curved her hand around the back of his neck, bringing his lips to hers. "Darling, *fair* is where you take your hog to win blue ribbons."

THE EDITOR'S CORNER

The coming month brings to mind lions and lambs—not only because of the weather but also because of our six wonderful LOVESWEPTs. In these books you'll find fierce and feisty, warm and gentle characters who add up to a rich and exciting array of people whose stories of falling in love are enthralling.

Judy Gill starts things off this month with another terrific story in **KISS AND MAKE UP**, LOVESWEPT #678. He'd never been around when they were married, but now that Kat Waddell has decided to hire a nanny to help with the kids, her ex-husband, Rand, insists he's perfect for the job! Accepting his offer means letting him live in the basement apartment—too dangerously close for a man whose presence arouses potent memories of reckless passion . . . and painful images of love gone wrong. He married Kat hoping for the perfect fantasy family, but the pretty picture he'd imagined didn't include an unhappy wife he never seemed to satisfy . . . except in bed. Now Rand needs to show Kat he's changed. The sensual magic he weaves makes her feel cherished at last, but Kat wonders if it's enough to mend their broken vows. Judy's special touch makes this story of love reborn especially poignant.

It's on to Scotland for **LORD OF THE ISLAND**, LOVESWEPT #679, by the wonderfully talented Kimberli Wagner. Ian MacLeod is annoyed by the American woman who comes to stay on Skye during the difficult winter months, but when Tess Hartley sheds her raingear, the laird is enchanted by the dark-eyed siren whose fiery temper reveals a rebel who won't be ordered around by any man—even him! He expects pity, even revulsion at the evidence of his terrible accident, but Tess's pain runs as deep as his does, and her artist's eye responds to Ian's scarred face with wonder at his courage . . . and a wildfire hunger to lose herself in his arms. As always, Kimberli weaves an intense story of love and triumph you won't soon forget.

Victoria Leigh gives us a hero who is rough, rugged, and capable of **DANGEROUS LOVE**, LOVESWEPT #680. Four years earlier, he'd fallen in love with her picture, but when Luke Sinclair arrives on her secluded island to protect his boss's sister from the man who'd once kidnapped her, he is stunned to find that Elisabeth Connor is more exquisite than he'd dreamed—and not nearly as fragile as he'd feared. Instead, she warms to the fierce heat of his gaze, begging to know the ecstacy of his touch. Even though he's sworn to protect her with his life, Elisabeth must make him see that she wants him to share it with her instead. Only Victoria could deliver a romance that's as sexy and fun as it is touching.

We're delighted to have another fabulous book from Laura Taylor this month, and **WINTER HEART**, LOVESWEPT #681, is Laura at her best. Suspicious that the elegant blonde has a hidden agenda when she hires him to restore a family mansion, Jack McMillan quickly puts Mariah Chandler on the defensive—and is shocked to feel a flash flood of heat and desire rush through him! He believes she is only a spoiled rich girl indulging a whim, but he can't deny the hunger that ignites within him to possess her. Tantalized by sensual longings she's never expected to feel, Mariah surrenders to the dizzying pleasure of Jack's embrace. She's fought her demons by helping other women who have suffered but has never told Jack of the shadows that still haunt her nights. Now Mariah must heal his wounded spirit by finally sharing her pain and daring him to share a future.

Debra Dixon brings together a hot, take-charge Cajun and a sizzling TV seductress in **MIDNIGHT HOUR,** LOVESWEPT #682. Her voice grabs his soul and turns him inside out before he even sees her, but when Dr. Nick Devereaux gazes at Midnight Mercy Malone, the town's TV horror-movie hostess, he aches to muss her gorgeous russet hair . . . and make love to the lady until she moans his name! Still, he likes her even better out of her slinky costumes, an everyday enchantress who tempts him to make regular house calls. His sexy accent gives her goosebumps, but Mercy hopes her lusty alter ego might scare off a man she fears will choose work over her. Yet, his kisses send her up in flames and make her ache for love that never ends. Debra's spectacular romance will leave you breathless.

Olivia Rupprecht invites you to a **SHOTGUN WEDDING,** LOVESWEPT #683. Aaron Breedlove once fled his mountain hamlet to escape his desire for Addy McDonald, but now fate has brought him back— and his father's deathbed plea has given him no choice but to keep the peace between the clans and marry his dangerous obsession! With hair as dark as a moonlit night, Addy smells of wildflowers and rainwater, and Aaron can deny his anguished passion no longer. He is the knight in shining armor she's always dreamed of, but Addy yearns to become his wife in every way—and

Aaron refuses to accept her gift or surrender his soul. **SHOTGUN WEDDING** is a sensual, steamy romance that Olivia does like no one else.

Happy reading,

With warmest wishes,

Nita Taublib

Nita Taublib

Associate Publisher

P.S. Don't miss the spectacular women's novels coming from Bantam in April: **DARK PARADISE** is the dangerously erotic novel of romantic suspense from nationally bestselling author Tami Hoag; **WARRIOR BRIDE** is a sizzling medieval romance in the bestselling tradition of Julie Garwood from Tamara Leigh, a dazzling new author; **REBEL IN SILK** is the fabulous new *Once Upon a Time* romance from bestselling Loveswept author Sandra Chastain. We'll be giving you a sneak peek at these terrific books in next month's LOVESWEPTs. And immediately following this page, look for a preview of the spectacular women's fiction books from Bantam *available now*!

Don't miss these exciting books by your favorite Bantam authors

On sale in February:
SILK AND STONE
by Deborah Smith

LADY DANGEROUS
by Suzanne Robinson

SINS OF INNOCENCE
by Jean Stone

"A uniquely significant voice in contemporary women's fiction."
—*Romantic Times*

Deborah Smith

SILK AND STONE

From Miracle *to* Blue Willow, *Deborah Smith's evocative novels have won a special place in readers' hearts. Now comes a spellbinding, unforgettably romantic new work. Vibrant with wit, aching with universal emotion,* SILK AND STONE *is Deborah Smith at her most triumphant . . .*

She had everything ready for him, everything but herself. What could she say to a husband she hadn't seen or spoken to in ten years: *Hi, honey, how'd your decade go?*

The humor was nervous, and morbid. She knew that. Samantha Raincrow hurt for him, hurt in ways she couldn't put into words. Ten years of waiting, of thinking about what he was going through, of *why* he'd been subjected to it, had worn her down to bare steel.

What he'd endured would always be her fault.

She moved restlessly around the finest hotel suite in the city, obsessed with straightening fresh flowers that were already perfectly arranged in their vases. He wouldn't have seen many flowers. She wanted him to remember the scent of youth and freedom. Of love.

Broad windows looked out over Raleigh. A nice city for a reunion. The North Carolina summer had just begun; the trees still wore the dark shades of new spring leaves.

She wanted everything to be new for him, but knew it could never be, that they were both haunted by the past—betrayals that couldn't be undone. She was Alexandra Lomax's niece; she couldn't scrub that stain out of her blood.

Her gifts were arranged around the suite's sitting room; Sam went to them and ran her hands over each one. A silk tapestry, six-feet-square and woven in geometrics from an old Cherokee design, was draped over a chair. She wanted him to see one of the ways she'd spent all the hours alone. Lined up in a precise row along one wall were five large boxes filled with letters she'd written to him and never sent, because he wouldn't have read them. A journal of every day. On a desk in front of the windows were stacks of bulging photo albums. One was filled with snapshots of her small apartment in California, the car she'd bought second-hand, years ago, and still drove, more of her tapestries, and her loom. And the Cove. Pictures of the wild Cove, and the big log house where he'd been born. She wanted him to see how lovingly she'd cared for it over the years.

The other albums were filled with her modeling portfolio. A strange one, by most standards. Just hands. Her hands, the only beautiful thing about her, holding soaps and perfumes and jewelry, caressing lingerie and detergent and denture cleaner, and a thousand other products. Because she wanted him to understand everything about her work, she'd brought the DeMeda book, too—page after over-sized, sensual page of black-and-white art photos. Photos of her fingertips touching a man's glistening, naked back, or molded to the crest of a muscular, bare thigh.

If he cared, she would explain about the ludicrous amount of money she'd gotten for that work, and that the book had been created by a famous photographer, and was considered an art form. If he cared, she'd assure him that there was nothing provocative about standing under hot studio lights with her hands cramping, while beautiful, half-clothed male models yawned and told her about their latest boyfriends.

If he cared.

Last, she went to a small, rectangular folder on a coffee table near the room's sofa. She sat down and opened it, her hands shaking so badly she could barely grasp the folder. The new deed for the Cove, with both his name and hers on it, was neatly tucked inside. She'd promised to transfer title to him the day he came home. If she hadn't held her ownership of the Cove over him like a threat all these years, he would have divorced her.

She hadn't promised to let him have it without her.

Sam hated that coercion, and knew he hated it, too. It was too much like something her Aunt Alexandra would have done. But Sam would not lose him, not without fighting for a second chance.

The phone rang. She jumped up, scattering the paperwork on the carpet, and ran to answer. "Dreyfus delivery service," said a smooth, elegantly drawling voice. "I have one slightly-used husband for you, ma'am."

Their lawyer's black sense of humor didn't help matters. Her heart pounded, and she felt dizzy. "Ben, you're downstairs?"

"Yes, in the lobby. Actually, I'm in the lobby. He's in the men's room, changing clothes."

"Changing clothes?"

"He asked me to stop on the way here. I perform many functions, Sam, but helping my clients pick a new outfit is a first."

"Why in the world—"

"He didn't want you to see him in what they gave him to wear. In a manner of speaking, he wanted to look like a civilian, again."

Sam inhaled raggedly and bowed her head, pressing her fingertips under her eyes, pushing hard. She wouldn't cry, wouldn't let him see her for the first time in ten years with her face swollen and her nose running. Small dignities were all she had left. "Has he said anything?" she asked, when she could trust herself to speak calmly.

"Hmmm, lawyer-client confidentiality, Sam. I represent both of you. What kind of lawyer do you think I am? Never mind, I don't want to hear the brutal truth."

"One who's become a good friend."

Ben hesitated. "Idle flattery." Then, slowly, "He said he would walk away without ever seeing you, again, if he could."

She gripped the phone numbly. *That's no worse than you expected,* she told herself. But she felt dead inside. "Tell him the doors to the suite will be open."

"All right. I'm sure he needs all the open doors he can get."

"I can't leave them all open. If I did, I'd lose him." Ben didn't ask what she meant; he'd helped her engineer some of those closed doors.

"Parole is not freedom," Ben said. "He understands that."

"And I'm sure he's thrilled that he's being forced to live with a wife he doesn't want."

"I suspect he doesn't know what he wants, at the moment."

"He's always known, Ben. That's the problem."

She said good-bye, put the phone down and walked with leaden resolve to the suite's double doors. She opened them and stepped back. For a moment, she considered checking herself in a mirror one last time, turned halfway, then realized she was operating on the assumption that what she looked like mattered to him. So she faced the doors and waited.

Each faint whir and rumble of the elevators down the hall made her nerves dance. She could barely breathe, listening for the sound of those doors opening. She smoothed her upswept hair, then anxiously fingered a blond strand that had escaped. Jerking at each hair, she pulled them out. A dozen or more, each unwilling to go. If it hurt, she didn't notice.

She clasped her hands in front of her pale yellow suitdress, then unclasped them, fiddled with the gold braid along the neck, twisted the plain gold wedding band on her left hand. She never completely removed it from her body, even when she worked. It had either remained on her finger or on a sturdy gold chain around her neck, all these years.

That chain, lying coldly between her breasts, also held his wedding ring.

She heard the hydraulic purr of an elevator settling into place, then the softer rush of metal doors sliding apart. Ten years compressed in the nerve-wracking space of a few seconds. If he weren't the one walking up the long hall right now, if some unsuspecting stranger strolled by instead, she thought her shaking legs would collapse.

Damn the thick carpeting. She couldn't gauge his steps. She wasn't ready. No, she would always be ready. Her life stopped, and she was waiting, waiting . . .

He walked into the doorway and halted. This tall, broad-shouldered stranger was her husband. Every memory she had of his appearance was there, stamped with a brutal decade of maturity, but there. Except for the look in his eyes. Nothing had ever been bleak and hard about him before. He stared at her with an intensity that could have burned her shadow on the floor.

Words were hopeless, but all that they had. "Welcome back," she said. Then, brokenly, "*Jake*."

He took a deep breath, as if a shiver had run through him. He closed the doors without ever taking his eyes off her. Then he was at her in two long steps, grasping her by the shoulders, lifting her to her toes. They were close enough to share a breath, a heartbeat. "I trained myself not to think about you," he said, his voice a raw whisper. "Because if I had, I would have lost my mind."

"I never deserted you. I wanted to be part of your life, but you wouldn't let me. Will you please try now?"

"Do you still have it?" he asked.

Anger. Defeat. The hoarse sound she made contained both. "Yes."

He released her. "Good. That's all that matters."

Sam turned away, tears coming helplessly. After all these years, there was still only one thing he wanted from her, and it was the one thing she hated, a symbol of pride and obsession she would never understand, a blood-red stone that had controlled the lives of too many people already, including theirs.

The Pandora ruby.

LADY DANGEROUS
by
Suzanne Robinson

"An author with star quality . . . spectacularly talented."
—Romantic Times

Liza Elliot had a very good reason for posing as a maid in the house of the notorious Viscount Radcliffe. It was the only way the daring beauty could discover whether this sinister nobleman had been responsible for her brother's murder. But Liza never knew how much she risked until the night she came face-to-face with the dangerously arresting and savagely handsome viscount himself . . .

Iron squealed against iron as the footmen swung the gates back again. Black horses trotted into view, two pairs, drawing a black lacquered carriage. Liza stirred uneasily as she realized that vehicle, tack, and coachman were all in unrelieved black. Polished brass lanterns and fittings provided the only contrast.

The carriage pulled up before the house, the horses stamping and snorting in the cold. The coachman, wrapped in a driving coat and muffled in a black scarf, made no sound as he controlled the ill-tempered menace of his animals. She couldn't help leaning forward a bit, in spite of her growing trepidation. Perhaps it was the eeriness of the fog-drenched night, or the unnerving appearance of the shining black and silent carriage, but no one moved.

Then she saw it. A boot. A black boot unlike any she'd ever seen. High of heel, tapered in the toe, scuffed, and sticking out of the carriage window. Its owner must be reclining inside. As she closed her mouth, which had fallen open, Liza saw a puff of smoke billow out from the interior. So aghast was she at this unorthodox arrival, she didn't hear the duke and his brother come down the steps to stand near her.

Suddenly the boot was withdrawn. The head footman immediately jumped forward and opened the carriage door. The interior lamps hadn't been lit. From the darkness stepped a man so tall, he had to curl almost double to keep his hat from hitting the roof of the vehicle.

The footman retreated as the man straightened. Liza sucked in her breath, and a feeling of unreality swamped her other emotions. The man who stood before her wore clothing so dark, he seemed a part of the night and the gloom of the carriage that had borne him. A low-crowned hat with a wide brim concealed his face, and he wore a long coat that flared away from his body. It was open, and he brushed one edge of it back where it revealed buckskin pants, a vest, a black, low-slung belt and holster bearing a gleaming revolver.

He paused, undisturbed by the shock he'd created. Liza suddenly remembered a pamphlet she'd seen on the American West. That's where she'd seen a man like this. Not anywhere in England, but in illustrations of the American badlands.

At last the man moved. He struck a match on his belt and lit a thin cigar. The tip glowed, and for a moment his face was revealed in the light of the match. She glimpsed black, black hair, so dark it seemed to absorb the flame of the match. Thick lashes lifted to reveal the glitter of cat-green eyes, a straight nose, and a chin that bore a day's stubble. The match died and was tossed aside. The man hooked his thumbs in his belt and sauntered down the line of servants, ignoring them.

He stopped in front of the duke, puffed on the cigar, and stared at the older man. Slowly, a pretense of a smile spread over his face. He removed the cigar from his mouth, shoved his hat back on his head, and spoke for the first time.

"Well, well, well. Evening, Daddy."

That accent, it was so strange—a hot, heavy drawl spiked with cool and nasty amusement. This man took his time with words, caressed them, savored them, and made his enemies wait in apprehension for him to complete them. The duke bristled, and his white hair almost stood out like a lion's mane as he gazed at his son.

"Jocelin, you forget yourself."

The cigar sailed to the ground and hissed as it hit the damp pavement. Liza longed to shrink back from the sudden viciousness that sprang from the viscount's eyes. The viscount smiled again and spoke softly, with relish and an evil amusement. The drawl vanished, to be supplanted by a clipped, aristocratic accent.

"I don't forget. I'll never forget. Forgetting is your vocation, one you've elevated to a sin, or you wouldn't bring my dear uncle where I could get my hands on him."

All gazes fastened on the man standing behind the duke. Though much younger than his brother, Yale Marshall had the same thick hair, black as his brother's had once been, only gray at the temples. Of high stature like his nephew, he reminded Liza of the illustrations of knights in *La Morte d'Arthur*, for he personified doomed beauty and chivalry. He had the same startling green eyes as his nephew, and he gazed at the viscount sadly as the younger man faced him.

Yale murmured to his brother, "I told you I shouldn't have come."

With knightly dignity he stepped aside, and the movement brought him nearer to his nephew. Jocelin's left hand touched the revolver on his hip as his uncle turned. The duke hissed his name, and the hand dropped loosely to his side. He lit another cigar.

At a glance from his face, the butler suddenly sprang into motion. He ran up the steps to open the door. The duke marched after him, leaving his son to follow, slowly, after taking a few leisurely puffs on his cigar.

"Ah, well," he murmured. "I can always kill him later."

SINS OF INNOCENCE
by
JEAN STONE

They were four women with only one thing in common: each gave up her baby to a stranger. They'd met in a home for unwed mothers, where all they had to hold on to was each other. Now, twenty-five years later, it's time to go back and face the past. The date is set for a reunion with the children they have never known. But who will find the courage to attend?

"I've decided to find my baby," Jess said.

Susan picked up a spoon and stirred in a hefty teaspoon of sugar from the bowl. She didn't usually take sugar, but she needed to keep her hands busy. Besides, if she tried to drink from the mug now, she'd probably drop it.

"What's that got to do with me?"

Jess took a sip, then quickly put down the mug. It's probably still too hot, Susan thought. She probably burned the Estée Lauder right off her lips.

"I . . ." The woman stammered, not looking Susan in the eye, "I was wondering if you've ever had the same feelings."

The knot that had found its way into Susan's stomach increased in size.

"I have a son," Susan said.

Jess looked into her mug. "So do I. In fact, I have two sons and a daughter. And"—she picked up the mug to try again—"a husband."

Susan pushed back her hair. *My* baby, she thought. *David's baby.* She closed her eyes, trying to envision what he would look like today. He'd be a man. Older even than David had been when . . .

How could she tell Jess that 1968 had been the biggest regret of her life? How could she tell this woman she no longer knew that she felt the decisions she'd made then had led her in a direction that had no definition, no purpose? But years ago Susan had accepted one important thing: She couldn't go back.

"So why do you want to do this?"

Jess looked across the table at Susan. "Because it's time," she said.

Susan hesitated before asking the next question. "What do you want from me?"

Jess set down her mug and began twisting the ring again. "Haven't you ever wondered? About your baby?"

Only a million times. Only every night when I go to bed. Only every day as I've watched Mark grow and blossom. Only every time I see a boy who is the same age.

"What are you suggesting?"

"I'm planning a reunion. With our children. I've seen Miss Taylor, and she's agreed to help. She knows where they all are."

"*All* of them?"

"Yours. Mine. P.J.'s and Ginny's. I'm going to

contact everyone, even the kids. Whoever shows up, shows up. Whoever doesn't, doesn't. It's a chance we'll all be taking, but we'll be doing it together. *Together*. The way we got through it in the first place."

The words hit Susan like a rapid fire of a BB gun at a carnival. She stood and walked across the room. She straightened the stack of laundry. "I think you're out of your mind," she said.

And don't miss these heart-stopping
romances from Bantam Books,
on sale in March:

DARK PARADISE
by the nationally bestselling author
Tami Hoag
"Tami Hoag belongs at the top of
everyone's favorite author list"
—*Romantic Times*

WARRIOR BRIDE
by **Tamara Leigh**
" . . . a passionate love story that captures all
the splendor of the medieval era."
—nationally bestselling author
Teresa Medeiros

REBEL IN SILK
by **Sandra Chastain**
"Sandra Chastain's characters' steamy
relationships are the stuff dreams are
made of."
—*Romantic Times*

SYDNEY OMARR

Now, the world's most knowledgeable astrologer, author of many books, and internationally acclaimed syndicated columnist reveals secrets about your...

THE MOST ACCURATE, IN-DEPTH FORECAST AVAILABLE BY PHONE!

- Personal Relationships
- Financial Outlook
- Career & Work
- Travel Plans
- Immediate Future
- Family
- Friends
- Dreams
- Love
- Money

Millions of people look to Sydney Omarr every day for their personal forecasts. Now, you too can have a customized extended weekly forecast from America's #1 Astrologer! Cast exclusively for your time, date and place of birth, this is the most accurate, most reliable, most in-depth personalized astrology forecast available by phone!

WEEKLY PREDICTIONS FROM AMERICA'S #1 ASTROLOGER!

1-900-903-3000
Only $1.50 Per Min. • Avg. Length Of Call 6 Min.

Call 24 hours a day, 7 days a week. You must be 18 yrs. or older to call and have a touch tone phone.

DHS1 7/93

OFFICIAL RULES

To enter the sweepstakes below carefully follow all instructions found elsewhere in this offer.

The **Winners Classic** will award prizes with the following approximate maximum values: 1 Grand Prize: $26,500 (or $25,000 cash alternate); 1 First Prize: $3,000; 5 Second Prizes: $400 each; 35 Third Prizes: $100 each; 1,000 Fourth Prizes: $7.50 each. Total maximum retail value of Winners Classic Sweepstakes is $42,500. Some presentations of this sweepstakes may contain individual entry numbers corresponding to one or more of the aforementioned prize levels. To determine the Winners, individual entry numbers will first be compared with the winning numbers preselected by computer. For winning numbers not returned, prizes will be awarded in random drawings from among all eligible entries received. Prize choices may be offered at various levels. If a winner chooses an automobile prize, all license and registration fees, taxes, destination charges and, other expenses not offered herein are the responsibility of the winner. If a winner chooses a trip, travel must be complete within one year from the time the prize is awarded. Minors must be accompanied by an adult. Travel companion(s) must also sign release of liability. Trips are subject to space and departure availability. Certain black-out dates may apply.

The following applies to the sweepstakes named above:

No purchase necessary. You can also enter the sweepstakes by sending your name and address to: P.O. Box 508, Gibbstown, N.J. 08027. Mail each entry separately. Sweepstakes begins 6/1/93. Entries must be received by 12/30/94. Not responsible for lost, late, damaged, misdirected, illegible or postage due mail. Mechanically reproduced entries are not eligible. All entries become property of the sponsor and will not be returned.

Prize Selection/Validations: Selection of winners will be conducted no later than 5:00 PM on January 28, 1995, by an independent judging organization whose decisions are final. Random drawings will be held at 1211 Avenue of the Americas, New York, N.Y. 10036. Entrants need not be present to win. Odds of winning are determined by total number of entries received. Circulation of this sweepstakes is estimated not to exceed 200 million. All prizes are guaranteed to be awarded and delivered to winners. Winners will be notified by mail and may be required to complete an affidavit of eligibility and release of liability which must be returned within 14 days of date on notification or alternate winners will be selected in a random drawing. Any prize notification letter or any prize returned to a participating sponsor, Bantam Doubleday Dell Publishing Group, Inc., its participating divisions or subsidiaries, or the independent judging organization as undeliverable will be awarded to an alternate winner. Prizes are not transferable. No substitution for prizes except as offered or as may be necessary due to unavailability, in which case a prize of equal or greater value will be awarded. Prizes will be awarded approximately 90 days after the drawing. All taxes are the sole responsibility of the winners. Entry constitutes permission (except where prohibited by law) to use winners' names, hometowns, and likenesses for publicity purposes without further or other compensation. Prizes won by minors will be awarded in the name of parent or legal guardian.

Participation: Sweepstakes open to residents of the United States and Canada, except for the province of Quebec. Sweepstakes sponsored by Bantam Doubleday Dell Publishing Group, Inc., (BDD), 1540 Broadway, New York, NY 10036. Versions of this sweepstakes with different graphics and prize choices will be offered in conjunction with various solicitations or promotions by different subsidiaries and divisions of BDD. Where applicable, winners will have their choice of any prize offered at level won. Employees of BDD, its divisions, subsidiaries, advertising agencies, independent judging organization, and their immediate family members are not eligible.

Canadian residents, in order to win, must first correctly answer a time limited arithmetical skill testing question. Void in Puerto Rico, Quebec and wherever prohibited or restricted by law. Subject to all federal, state, local and provincial laws and regulations. For a list of major prize winners (available after 1/29/95): send a self-addressed, stamped envelope entirely separate from your entry to: Sweepstakes Winners, P.O. Box 517, Gibbstown, NJ 08027. Requests must be received by 12/30/94. DO NOT SEND ANY OTHER CORRESPONDENCE TO THIS P.O. BOX.

SWP 7/93

Don't miss these fabulous Bantam women's fiction titles

Now on Sale

● **SILK AND STONE** by Deborah Smith

From MIRACLE to BLUE WILLOW, Deborah Smith's evocative novels won a special place in reader's hearts. Now, from the author hailed by critics as "a uniquely significant voice in contemporary women's fiction," comes a spellbinding, unforgettably romantic new work. Vibrant with wit, aching with universal emotion, SILK AND STONE is Deborah Smith at her most triumphant.

___29689-2 $5.99/$6.99 in Canada

● **LADY DANGEROUS**
by Suzanne Robinson

Liza Elliot had a very good reason for posing as a maid in the house of the notorious Viscount Radcliffe. It was the only way the daring beauty could discover whether this sinister nobleman had been responsible for her brother's murder. But Liza never knew how much she risked until the night she came face-to-face with the dangerously arresting and savagely handsome viscount himself.

___29576-4 $5.50/$6.50 in Canada

● **SINS OF INNOCENCE**
by Jean Stone

They were four women with only one thing in common: each gave up her baby to a stranger. They'd met in a home for unwed mothers, where all they had to hold on to was each other. Now, twenty-five years later, it's time to go back and face the past.

___56342-4 $5.99/$6.99 n Canada

Ask for these books at your local bookstore or use this page to order.

❑ Please send me the books I have checked above. I am enclosing $ _____ (add $2.50 to cover postage and handling). Send check or money order, no cash or C. O. D.'s please.

Name _____

Address _____

City/ State/ Zip _____

Send order to: Bantam Books, Dept. FN134, 2451 S. Wolf Rd., Des Plaines, IL 60018
Allow four to six weeks for delivery.
Prices and availability subject to change without notice.

FN 134 3/94

Don't miss these fabulous Bantam women's fiction titles

On Sale in March

● DARK PARADISE

by Tami Hoag, the nationally bestselling author of *CRY WOLF*

"Ms Hoag is...a writer of superlative talent." —Romantic Times

Enter into a thrilling tale where a murderer lurks and death abounds. And where someone has the power to turn a slice of heaven into a dark paradise.

_____56161-8 $5.99/$7.50 in Canada

● WARRIOR BRIDE

by Tamara Leigh

"Fresh, exciting...wonderfully sensual...sure to be noticed in the romance genre."—New York Times *bestselling author Amanda Quick*

Ranulf Wardieu was furious to discover his jailer was a raven-haired maiden garbed in men's clothing and skilled in combat. But he vowed that he would storm her defenses with sweet caresses and make his captivating enemy his..

_____56533-8 $5.50/6.99 in Canada

● REBEL IN SILK

by Sandra Chastain

"Sandra Chastain's characters' steamy relationships are the stuff dreams are made of."—Romantic Times

Dallas Burke had come to Willow Creek, Wyoming, to find her brother's killer, and she had no intention of being scared off—not by the roughnecks who trashed her newspaper office, nor by the devilishly handsome cowboy who stole her heart.

_____56464-1 $5.50/6.99 in Canada

Ask for these books at your local bookstore or use this page to order.

❑ Please send me the books I have checked above. I am enclosing $ _____ (add $2.50 to cover postage and handling). Send check or money order, no cash or C. O. D.'s please.

Name _____

Address _____

City/ State/ Zip _____

Send order to: Bantam Books, Dept. FN135, 2451 S. Wolf Rd., Des Plaines, IL 60018

Allow four to six weeks for delivery.

Prices and availability subject to change without notice.

FN135 3/94